# YETI FOR LOVE

## ALASKA YETI SERIES
## BOOK 3

## NEVA POST

ICICLE INK, LLC

Created with Vellum

# CONTENT NOTICE

Hello monster lover, I'm so glad you are here!

Before we get started, I want to warn you that the hero in this book, Dorje, is dealing with the loss of his grandmother and loss because of a mountaineering accident. Both incidents happen off page, over a year before this story takes place. If you are grieving for a friend or loved one or have experienced a tragedy in the wilderness or elsewhere, my sincere condolences. While Yeti for Love is mostly a flirty story about a wanderlust who meets a sexy yeti, there are aspects of the book that might not be for you right now. Use your best judgement and take care. - Neva

*In memory of Karo.*

**A yeti ice climbing instructor who's too hot for his harness.**

In search of a new adventure, Gina moves to the frosty wilds of Alaska. She never expected to fall helmet over crampons for Dorje—*a yeti*—whose hotness could melt glaciers. He possesses mad climbing skills, a penchant for baking, and the ability to sweep her off her feet. In Dorje, Gina realizes she's found her ultimate adventure.

**A free spirit who sparkles like fresh snow.**

Dorje copes with recent loss by knitting and binging telenovelas. As his yarn budget dwindles, he reluctantly returns to work, teaching charismatic newbie Gina to ice climb. When he accidentally reveals his yeti secret, she doesn't scream and run. She invites him to dinner. Gina is strong, confident and brings the first smile to his face in over a year.

Gina can now conquer a frozen waterfall, but can she scale the walls around Dorje's heart and convince him that life is better when they're roped together?

# CHAPTER ONE

**D**orje relaxed deeper into his couch. The over-the-top drama of a Spanish-language telenovela played out on his television screen, while the gentle slide of bamboo knitting needles soothed his nerves. The repetitive motions set the same calming tone as it had last night, last week—the whole last year.

He deftly worked a needle under the taut yarn braced against a tender spot on his large, azure finger. Calluses were common, or so he'd learned through online forums. But the finger protectors his fellow knitters had recommended were too small for a yeti—not that they knew what he was.

Dorje's eyes were following the subtitles when his string slackened. Ten stitches to the end of the row, a foot short of the pattern length, and he'd run out of yarn. Again.

He capped his needle and adjusted his stitch counter before crossing the room to a cedar chest containing a sizable yarn stash left to him by Nana, his late human grandmother. But when Dorje lifted the lid, he found only small, leftover balls.

He turned to a growing pile of knitted goods next to the chest and lifted two—no, three—finished baby blankets. Six caps in a silky synthetic that would keep bare heads warm. A few pairs of child-size mittens, complete with connector strings. And beneath those were three shawls—er, make that five.

Case of the missing skeins solved. He'd used the Wooly Wonder on new shawls. He'd depleted Nana's yarn stash.

He should have been proud of the stack he'd amassed for the Groundhog-Be-Damned Knit-a-thon, but it wasn't enough. His products would help cancer patients, foster children, and the retirement center residents in Wildwood, Alaska, where Nana had spent her last years.

A familiar panic gripped Dorje, and he squeezed his eyes shut.

*Do more.*

*Try harder.*

*Succeed this time.*

It had nothing to do with needles and yarn, and everything to do with the unrecovered body now forever entombed in Black Rock Glacier's ice.

Images flashed behind his lids. Blinding snow and the sting of icy wind. Roping up. An injured person within reach. As his chest tightened, he forced out a long, slow breath.

More than a year had passed. Would he remain broken forever? *Why can't I get over this?*

Dorje returned to the couch, slumping back as he rubbed his temples. When he opened his eyes, his gaze fell on Nana's picture, and a hollow sadness enveloped him. She'd died shortly before the unrelated climbing accident. He'd undertaken this knitting project in her memory and to overcome the feelings of failure that threatened to swallow him whole.

Before panic seized him again, Dorje picked up his phone. Over the last year, he'd mostly used it to look up patterns and message fellow knitters.

He swiped his employer's number—at least he *hoped* Mountain High Guiding Service still employed him. He hadn't talked to his boss, Denzin, since taking a leave of absence after the accident. Denzin served as Regional Manager, impressive for a yeti, especially since he had to attend meetings virtually and without video.

Given the late hour, Dorje readied himself to leave a message. But a voice sounded at the other end of the line. "Dorje?"

It took Dorje a moment to overcome his surprise and respond. "Hey, Eddie." He paused, frowning. "You never answer Mountain High's phone—or even your own phone. Where's Denzin?"

"I answer my phone. Sometimes," Eddie grumbled. "Denzin and Toni are out of town. He and Tseten said you're participating in a knitting, uh, event. Did you get Mountain High's pledge?"

Tseten, a fellow yeti, had been a loyal friend this past year. "I did, thanks. The pledges go straight to the charities I selected." He cleared his throat. "But I could use a paycheck to replenish my yarn stash. Do you have any jobs I could pick up?"

Eddie responded quickly. "You want to come back to work?" His surprised tone made Dorje wince.

"Not a big guiding trip. I'm not ready for that. Something small, close to Wildwood."

"Someone called today requesting private ice climbing lessons. Hang on." Static sounded on the line, like the microphone scraped across clothing as

Eddie moved his phone around. "Can you hear me?" he asked, his voice more distant. "Got you on speaker while I look up this email."

A smile tugged at Dorje's mouth. The movement felt foreign, but pleasant. "Congrats on not disconnecting the call."

Eddie might be human, but he had no problem producing a growl. "Shove it, Dorj."

"Apologies," Dorje continued, biting back a laugh.

"You're not sorry," Eddie said in an exasperated tone. "I don't do technology. That's why I'm a guide. You want to climb a mountain? Build a snow cave? I'm your guy. Managing emails and answering phones? Not how I wish to spend the bulk of my time."

Eddie went silent as he navigated the phone. After several moments, he said, "Got it. Gina from Wildwood would like ice climbing lessons. Has no experience, but wants to start immediately."

"Does she know about yeti?" Few humans knew yeti existed—even within Wildwood. The public's discovery could threaten their safety and autonomy. All yeti avoided exposing themselves and the greater yeti community.

Eddie let out a sigh. "No, I don't think so."

It didn't mean that Dorje couldn't accept the job, but he'd have to take precautions. Aside from that, this sounded perfect. Close to home. Short-term. And a low-risk activity—a beginner wouldn't start on big, dangerous ice. "I'll suit up."

"Hat, face cover, gloves?"

"And goggles. Tell her I have a skin condition."

"Right. I'll send her your bio and contact info. If she's okay with the pairing, she'll be in touch."

Dorje grunted. "Thanks, I appreciate the opportunity."

A silent beat passed. "It's good to hear from you, Dorje," Eddie said before disconnecting.

Dorje clicked off his phone. He sat back and glanced around the room, his gaze landing on the paused telenovela and the items he'd made.

If he didn't need the paycheck to buy more yarn, he wouldn't have reached out to Mountain High. He'd made a commitment and local charities were counting on him. He couldn't make good on his promise without a knitting allowance. He'd failed in the wilderness last winter, but this job would be different. Teaching a beginner was the best way to dip his toes back in the water.

Though nervous as hell, an excited flutter coursed through him at the thought of getting back outside to resume his role as guide and instructor. He could do this. And he'd start with a human named Gina.

GINA JOGGED along a snowy trail toward the Wildwood Retirement Center. She could have walked, but she had way too much energy to burn. Spring was still three weeks away, according to the calendar, but the sun shone brightly, glittering off the snow, and slowly melting icicles on the building eaves. She might be a newbie to Alaska, but cabin fever was real, and Gina couldn't get enough gorgeous March days.

Pushing her sunglasses atop her head, she pulled open the retirement center's front door and stomped her boots to knock off loose snow. Her work as an online tutor meant she could set her own schedule and spend time outdoors or have tea with her new friend Mari on a weekday afternoon.

As she walked into the cafeteria where Mari worked, Gina's phone buzzed with a text and music blared. She scrambled to wrestle the device from her coat pocket. Too late. The tune repeated itself. Loudly.

Mari stood alone in the room, hands sliding to her hips as the song ended. An amused smile played at her lips. "The Indiana Jones theme song? Really? Don't tell me that's Adventure Ted's ringtone."

Heat flashed up the back of Gina's neck. In winter, her sun-starved freckles didn't hide the raspberry-red blush spreading across her pale skin. But she lifted her chin and shrugged. "It was free, and it fits him."

"Is he still calling you *Nina*?" She emphasized the "N."

It probably wasn't a good sign that he kept getting her name wrong, especially when she'd corrected him more than once. But she didn't care. She needed a friend. "Maybe his phone is autocorrecting my name in texts."

"Right," she said, not sounding convinced. "And he's on his way to Alaska?"

Gina skipped to her chair in her excitement. "Yes, he's driving up. I can't wait!" She loved Wildwood, but had only met a few people. She had the sense that she was missing out and often felt like an outsider in the community, despite the friendly nature of most people she'd met. However, Ted planned to visit over spring break—just two weeks away. She'd have someone other than Mari to hang out with. Someone to join her outside and share in adventures.

Mari led Gina to a table where she'd placed a kettle, mugs, and a selection of tea bags. "Remind me again how you met this guy?" Mari asked.

Gina plucked an herbal packet from the mix. "In Colorado, over winter break when I visited my sister Emma and her boyfriend." A burst of mint hit the air as she tore the packet open. "Adventure Ted and I bonded over ramen in a little food chalet at the ski resort. We have a mutual friend, so I know he's not a serial killer."

The plastic honey bear wheezed as Mari squeezed a spoonful into her mug. "And he introduced himself as 'Adventure Ted'? Not Ted? Not 'some people call me Adventure Ted'?"

Not only had he introduced himself that way, but he'd entered himself in Gina's phone contacts as Adventure Ted, under A for Adventure. She chose not to share that detail.

"It might sound weird, but he was all smiles, deep dimples, and charming. Just wait until you meet him. He draws people to him." Gina sipped her tea, then added, "And his name comes from all his experiences. He's done so many cool things, like backpack through Europe—"

"Many people have," Mari cut in dryly.

"Hiked the Inca Trail."

"Tour package."

"Trekked through Nepal."

"We haven't known each other long, so I might be out of line, but be careful, Gina. You don't know this guy well. I don't want you to get hurt. Don't let your fear of missing out get you in trouble by breaking your heart or fracturing your leg up on a mountain."

"I appreciate your concern." Gina set her mug on the table and let out a chuckle. "Yes, I have FOMO. Sometimes I act first and think later if I believe I'm missing an opportunity, but I won't take any unnecessary risks. I'll be fine." She paused and let out a heavy sigh. "I've met plenty of people in Wildwood this past year, but . . . I'm lonely. I look forward to visiting and taking him ice climbing—"

Mari sputtered into her tea. "Wait, does he still think you ice climb?"

"I didn't correct him when he assumed I knew." A smug smile tugged at Gina's lips as she leaned back, cradling her mug. "But I *will* know how to ice climb when Adventure Ted arrives."

"Can we just call him Ted?"

"Not to his face."

Mari crossed her arms. "Okay then. So you're learning to ice climb?"

"My lessons start tomorrow. I hired Mountain High Guiding Service like you recommended." She swirled her tea. "I can't wait. I have four sessions planned, Tuesday and Thursday this week and next. Then Ted arrives."

Mari's lips pressed together as she worried the slim gold chain around her neck. "Will Eddie be your instructor?"

Gina shook her head. "I talked to him, but I'm working with Dorje."

Mari swallowed her tea the wrong way and began coughing. "It's pronounced DOR-GEE." she wheezed. "Eddie said Dorje would teach your lessons?"

Getting someone's name right was important— Gina would know. She mouthed the correct pronunciation before responding. "Yeah, Dorje and I texted." Gina glanced at her phone. "I'm meeting him tomorrow at Lower Fireweed Falls. Why, do you know him?"

Mari's eyes seemed wider than normal as she slowly nodded. "I do. Did, uh, Eddie say anything else?"

A weird question. "I . . . Well, he said Dorje has a

skin condition he's sensitive about, so he might cover his face. Is that what you mean?"

Mari grimaced. "Sorta," she said. But then her frown lines eased, and she smiled in earnest. "Dorje is a nice guy. His grandmother lived here at the retirement center before she died. He's had a tough year though, and I'm glad to hear he's working again."

Gina leaned forward. "Should I be concerned?"

"No, you'll be in expert hands. He's one of the best."

A pulse of excitement shot through Gina at that news. *One of the best! Squee!* She *had* always suffered from FOMO. That's what had brought her to Alaska. She'd never in a million years introduce herself as Adventure Gina, but she did secretly think of herself that way. Where her twin sister Emma followed a boring and predictable path in life, Gina traipsed in whatever direction her heart desired.

"I have gear you can borrow, if you need it," Mari offered.

Gina accepted and practically vibrated in her seat as they finished visiting. She'd soon be an ice climber and have her friend Ted in Wildwood. And now that she had lessons lined up, she couldn't wait to meet Dorje and get started on a new adventure.

## CHAPTER TWO

G ina faced a decision the next morning after a last-minute cancellation by an online pupil. She could use the extra time to grade assignments, or she could test her borrowed crampons and tools *before* her ice climbing lesson began.

She imagined herself sinking an ice axe into a frozen waterfall . . . Yeah, grading could wait.

The Lower Fireweed Falls trailhead sat empty when Gina pulled in forty-five minutes early. After yanking on the old, stiff boots Mari had loaned her, Gina awkwardly walked around her car to her open hatchback. Her teal and orange snowsuit—a sweet retro find from her parent's closet before she moved to Alaska—swished with her clumsy steps.

The trunk seemed the safest spot in the car for

sharp, pointy things like the crampons and ice axes. She'd attached both to the outside of her backpack. Inside, she'd stored an extra layer of clothes and energy bars. No one liked a hangry outdoor partner.

Grinning, she shouldered her pack and thumped across the pullout, skirting the guardrail to follow a narrow path beat into the snow.

The trail descended from the parking lot to nearly level ground at the base of the waterfalls— likely a shallow pool in summer. A thin trace of new snow covered the area, but she assumed it concealed ice underneath.

Gina perched on a downed cottonwood tree at the edge of the frozen creek to attach crampons to her boots. She immediately caught her cuff on metal prongs and ripped a small hole right through her retro getup. *Dang it!* After disentangling from the pointy teeth, she placed the sharp side down into the snow. She did the same with the other crampon before sliding her feet between the straps and securing the buckles.

Next, Gina unclipped a climbing helmet from her pack and placed it on her head, but it didn't fit over her chunky hat's faux fur pompom. She removed her hat and shoved it into her pack, then improvised, folding her neck gaiter in two before sliding it up to cover her ears. The helmet fit well after the switch.

Gripping an ice axe in each hand, Gina took a tentative step in the crampons. The spikes dug into the solid creek and her footing felt secure.

The frozen waterfall wasn't smooth ice, but white undulating mounds. She walked up to the face and swung her axe. It sunk into the wall in the most satisfying way, but her grin fell when she tried to remove it. She had to drop the other axe and yank it out using both hands. Apparently, there was an art to this.

She swung the axe again, embedding the tip into the ice with a thwack. Next, she kicked the solid mass with her toe and buried the lethal-looking spikes. Gina tentatively rested her weight on the foot lodged about six inches up the wall. It held. *Yes!* She swung her other axe, and this time put weight on that too, using it to hoist herself up as she kicked her other foot into the wall.

She repeated this several more times. *Kick, kick, swing, pull.* It may not have been graceful, but she loved the rhythm as she moved up the ice. She pictured doing this with Ted. By the time he arrived, she'd have experience, have advanced beyond this beginner waterfall that only stretched forty feet from bottom to top.

A vehicle door slammed shut in the parking area above Gina, pulling her out of her daydream. Her focus had been up—the top of the falls—but now she looked down, and her stomach dropped faster than a bad carnival ride. She'd climbed higher than she'd realized, nearly halfway up the frozen curtain.

Her right knee shook with nerves. Stupid FOMO—made her way too impulsive. Why hadn't she waited for Dorje, for an actual lesson? Gina let out a slow breath to calm herself. If she could go up, surely she could go down.

Since her legs weren't steady, she first drew her right axe out of the ice, lowered it, and tried to sink it back in. But it wasn't the same movement as reaching up to swing. She couldn't get any leverage. The tip bounced off the frozen surface, and she almost dropped it.

Gina once again swung the tool above her head anchoring it. She needed both arms and legs securing her while she figured out what to do.

As she surveyed her situation, a deep voice rumbled above her. "Hey there."

She looked up to see a bulky figure peering over the top of the falls. They wore large, reflective ski goggles over their eyes, and a blue gaiter covered the rest of their face. A deep-blue helmet peeked from under the hood of their jade-green jacket. No skin showing. Her instructor. "Dorje?" She'd squeaked his name as her nerves got the better of her. *Damn it.*

He gave a nod. "Are you Gina?"

She tried to sound cheerful. "That's me. Great to meet you. I, um, thought I'd get a head start." Her voice came out uneven and shaky, as if she were driving over a washboard gravel road.

A news headline flashed in her mind. *Instructor witnesses overeager beginner shatter both legs in ice climbing fall.*

She'd hoped to make a new friend in Dorje—assuming she made it through the afternoon. So much for a good first impression.

———

DORJE'S GUT clenched at the waver in Gina's voice. Her smile resembled a grimace, and her green eyes reminded him of stormy ocean waves.

He'd arrived early to spread out gear so he could explain each piece of equipment—and have a moment to control his nerves. No time for that now. He'd either sink or swim.

Instead of giving in to the threatening panic, he forced himself to stay levelheaded. "I thought you were a novice. May I ask if you're comfortable solo climbing?"

A strangled giggle bubbled out of her mouth as she eyed the ground a good twenty feet below her. "This is my first time ice climbing," she admitted. "I got myself in over my head."

Another burst of nervous laughter popped out. "Turns out that climbing down is harder than up. Is the waterfall stretching on either end? Seems like I'm getting farther from the bottom and still nowhere near the top."

Dorje didn't chide. He needed her to remain calm and confident. Given the situation, she'd need to descend before her muscles tired. Her risk of serious injury decreased with each step down—less distance to fall. The higher she climbed, the greater the potential drop. "Focus on your breath, Gina."

She nodded, plump pink lips pursing as she blew out a slow breath.

"Try to relax. You're not that far from the bottom. You'll be down in no time. I'm going to grab my gear. I'll be below you in just a minute. In the meantime, try to hang from straight arms. Let your skeleton take your weight instead of your muscles."

She gave a quick nod before letting out another measured breath. This time, her gaze conveyed trust and confidence. It felt misplaced, but he wouldn't consider letting her down.

Dorje flew to his truck and grabbed his pack. Gina wasn't too far off the ground, but a fall with sharp tools onto hard ice was dangerous and there wasn't much time before she tired. He vaulted over the guardrail like an Olympian over a hurdle, landing halfway down the short trail to the base of the falls. He covered the remaining distance in a few strides.

It wouldn't do to skitter out onto the icy creek without crampons. He needed to be as stable as possible to assist in her descent. He checked in with her as he strapped the metal spikes to his boots. "How you doing, Gina?" His gut rioted, but his tone remained calm and even.

"Hanging in there," she said. Then added, "Ha, joking."

He didn't laugh but gave her a reassuring smile before remembering she couldn't see his face, thanks to the neck gaiter he'd secured under his goggles. She watched him, looking down through the crook of her elbow as he approached the base of the falls. "Okay, Gina," he said, speaking her name again to keep her engaged, let her know he was there for her, focused on her. "I'm going to talk you through climbing down."

She nodded, her tongue darting out to moisten her lips. "I'm ready."

"Look at the ice about a foot or so down from each hand and find the divots left by your ice axe as you climbed up."

He watched as she scanned the uneven surface to her right and left. A sudden bright smile conveyed her results before she responded, "I think I see them."

"Good job."

Her smile widened at his praise, and he felt his lips lift in response. He liked the effect his words had on her, though the real work hadn't started. "Now," he said, "I want you to slide one arm down until you can anchor the tip of your axe into that notch."

She slowly did as he instructed, leaving most of her weight on her toes, relying on the anchored axe in her other hand.

"Are you able to put your weight on that hold?" he asked. When her helmet bobbed in a nod, he said, "You're doing great. It's time to lower your feet. Pull one foot out and kick in a few inches below where you're at now."

On a long exhale, Gina followed his direction,

lowering herself a short distance. With his guidance, she repeated the steps, bit by bit, getting closer, until he could reach up and grasp her ankle.

"Almost down, Gina. You're doing an excellent job." Through all the layers of clothing, he gave her lower leg a slight squeeze. "Is my touch okay?"

She let out a gusty breath. "Like a lifejacket. Don't let go of me."

He wouldn't. He raised his other arm, his hands sliding against her legs as she lowered herself down a few inches at a time.

She was making excellent progress when he froze. She hadn't looped her wrists through the ice axe straps. A jolt of adrenaline flooded Dorje's body as his heart rate spiked. Though many people climbed without them, it meant that she could have lost a tool at any moment and fallen to the base of the falls.

A flash of last winter's failed rescue played out in Dorje's mind. Blowing snow. Roping up and lowering into an icy crevasse. He squeezed his eyes shut and blinked them open to focus on the here and now. He called up to Gina and, for the first time, his voice sounded unsteady, unconfident. The tone belied all the weakness and failure he'd felt since last year. He hated it.

As if he'd transferred his unease to her, one axe tip wobbled. It popped out of the divot, and she lost her grip. "Shit, watch out!" she cried.

He dodged the falling tool and gave himself a mental shake. This was not last year. This was Fireweed Falls and his new client, whom he would not let down. Dorje widened his legs as he prepared to catch her. "I've got you," he said in the strongest voice he could muster as he went up on his toes and wrapped his hands around her upper legs.

He plucked Gina from the wall, lowering her until she connected with his chest, her body cradled in his arms. "I've got you," he repeated.

She was safe now. He had her.

"It's okay," he said, as if trying to convince himself.

## CHAPTER THREE

Strong, solid arms held Gina. Dorje was every bit the safety net she'd imagined him to be. He'd grabbed her like a running back cradling a football for a touchdown. But her crampons had snagged on the ice. Her legs stuck straight out, wedged into the frozen falls as she leaned back into him. It was just as well that she wasn't on her feet. Her legs might not support her weight right now.

He'd been so calm, so reassuring until the end. She'd done something wrong—more wrong than climbing without a partner or harness and rope. There'd been doubt in that deep, rumbly voice of his. She'd internalized it, causing the ice axe to bobble right out of her shaking hand as she questioned herself.

She melted into Dorje's arms as adrenaline drained from her limbs. He murmured, "It's okay," and "I've got you." His hushed words spoken near her ear wavered as he repeated them like a chant.

Her breath calmed. But his grip didn't ease. Her heart slowed while his drilled against her back like a woodpecker on steroids.

She couldn't budge in his unyielding grip. Part of her didn't want to leave his embrace. No one had held her in a long time. She'd imagined Ted holding her, but after being in these large, solid arms that hugged her so well, any other arms would disappoint.

However, all good things had to come to an end. She patted his forearm. "Dorje?"

He responded, "It's okay."

It clearly wasn't, but she agreed with him. "Yes, it *is* okay. Everything is okay now." She swallowed, then tried the same technique he'd used on her. "You did great, Dorje. I'm okay, and you're okay. We're both okay."

He hummed, then released a long exhale. Gradually his hold eased, and Gina placed her feet back on the ground. She pulled away from Dorje, then turned to take him in.

No wonder the ground still looked a mile below her when she'd fallen into his capable arms. He was freaking huge—at least seven feet tall and nearly as broad as two average men.

Despite his layers of clothing and covered face, Gina could tell that this giant suffered. He signaled he needed a moment, then sank to one knee.

Mari's words came back to her. She'd said that Dorje'd had a tough year and only recently started working again.

*I broke the instructor.* Gina squeezed her eyes shut. "I'm really, really sorry. I should not have come out here on my own. I get excited and ahead of myself. What I did was thoughtless. I-I hope we can still work together."

Dorje's neck gaiter went concave as he sucked in a breath, and Gina's heart squeezed. She wanted to right this wrong.

He nodded. "Same time tomorrow?" His voice held a fraction of the strength compared to when he'd talked her down the falls.

They didn't have another lesson scheduled until Thursday. Gina had a client booked at this time tomorrow. If she canceled, she didn't get paid.

But she took in Dorje. After today, she owed him. And an extra lesson would give her a chance to redeem herself. She'd make it up to the student later.

"I'd appreciate that," Gina said, offering Dorje a smile. "Let's start fresh tomorrow."

---

DORJE CRACKED a beer but set it on the side table, too agitated to drink or knit. Even his beloved telenovela couldn't hold his attention.

He let out a deep breath and lay back on the couch, arm resting over closed eyes. Today had been a lot. That woman—Gina. Making jokes as she hung from the frozen curtain of ice by a few metal points. She hadn't even had the ice axe leash around her wrists. She could have . . .

His breathing grew erratic as gruesome scenarios played out in his head. Dorje fought for calm. Nothing healthy would come from that train of thought. Gina had been strong. She'd made it down in one piece. And tomorrow they'd take a different approach—one that involved emphasis on the basics and safety.

Dorje's phone rang, pulling him from his thoughts. He reached over and plucked it from the side table. It was the Mountain High main line.

Gina had agreed to another lesson while they

were still at the waterfall. But what if she changed her mind and contacted Mountain High to have him fired? He'd nearly collapsed in front of her, after all.

Trepidation laced Dorje's voice as he answered. "Hey, Eddie."

Eddie didn't return a greeting. "What did you do, man?"

Dorje bolted upright, a sick feeling spreading through his middle. "What did she say? Did Gina request another instructor?"

"Another . . .? No. She wanted to pay for an extra lesson and got frustrated when I wouldn't let her include a tip with the payment. She said you earned it."

Dorje blinked, then on an exhale, he collapsed back. "Oh."

"Whatever you did, keep doing it," Eddie advised. He fell silent. They both did. Then he asked, "So, what did you do?"

Dorje hesitated. He didn't want to share the poor choices Gina had made. The others might judge her. No one was perfect. And despite everything, she'd stayed strong, been cheerful. With those bright red braids and that quick smile, she'd been a spark of light, even in a tough situation—of her own making.

But she hadn't told Eddie that the incident had brought Dorje to his knees, gasping for oxygen.

Dorje cleared his throat. "Like any responsible instructor, I supported the client."

Eddie paused. "Supported her? Okay . . . Keep up the good work, etcetera. I told Gina, your new biggest fan, to tip you in person or ask you about your charity."

"Oh, thanks. I . . . Wait. Fan?"

"Her praise was effusive. Gotta run, man." He quickly added, "Glad you're back and killing it."

The knots in Dorje's middle loosened as he disconnected, but his phone immediately rang again. Tseten. *Sweet summer snow*. Dorje hadn't talked to this many people in one day in over a year. Even when they'd taken him fishing last summer at his brother Yeshe's cabin, they'd let him mope and be silent.

Tseten was a good friend, occasionally hanging out this past year, even when Dorje hadn't uttered a word. But a one-sided phone call hardly worked.

Tseten got straight to the point when Dorje connected. "Hey, so I hear you rescued your new client today. How are you feeling?"

Dorje rolled his eyes. "First, I'm not going to

share my feelings, Tset. Second, how do you know about Gina?"

"Gina," he repeated, as if reminding himself of her name. "Right. Can't wait to meet her—if, er, she learns about yeti." Tseten's girlfriend lived in California, and she didn't know her long-distance sweetheart had blue skin and fluffy white fur. "Gina talked with Mari, then *I* talked with Mari."

Huh. Gina *had* shared what happened, and with someone he knew. "So Gina knows Mari?"

"Yeah, apparently they meet weekly for tea at the retirement center."

Dorje rubbed his temple, exhausted from all the social interaction. "About today. I'm . . . managing. But I can't talk, Tset." He promised the extrovert yeti that he'd introduce him to Gina *if* she ever learned about their kind, and then ended the call.

But Gina wouldn't learn about yeti, not if Dorje could help it. He'd teach her ice climbing basics, get paid, and then get back to knitting and his quiet, solitary life. Plus, her praise would dry up after she went through his planned safety course tomorrow. It didn't involve climbing ice at all.

He wasn't getting back at her. Safety was paramount. But withholding ice from Gina would be a small form of torture. After what she'd put him through today, he didn't feel bad. Dorje folded his arms behind his head, and a rusty smile tugged at his lips as he imagined Gina's reaction to his plans. She wouldn't be happy, but it would be for her own good.

## CHAPTER FOUR

The next day, Gina aimed to arrive after Dorje. She didn't want her instructor to wonder if she'd tried the ice again before their lesson. Gina waved as she turned into the Lower Fireweed Falls pullout.

Dorje stood at the back of his truck dressed the same as yesterday, skin totally covered. He appeared to be laying out climbing gear on the truck's tailgate, as if setting it up for display, and raised a gloved hand in greeting.

Gina tugged on a thin fleece hat—one that would fit under her helmet—and walked over to her instructor. "Morning, Dorje." She smiled up at him and saw her own reflection in his goggles. "Thank you for meeting me for an extra lesson. And . . ." She ducked her head feeling sheepish. "And for everything you did yesterday. I am sorry. I'm ready to learn how to do things the right way today."

"A fresh start, right?" he said. She could hear the smile in his voice.

"Exactly," she agreed with an exhale. She wanted to ask how he was, if he felt better. But it didn't seem in the spirit of a fresh start. Instead, she gestured to the gear he'd laid out on the truck's tailgate. "Let me grab my backpack too, and we can go down to the falls."

Gina spun to return to her car, but a large hand landed on her shoulder, stopping her. "You don't need your pack yet."

She turned. "But it has all my gear in it."

"We'll go over gear in a minute," he said lightly. "But I usually start with 'Thanks for choosing Mountain High.' Then I ask about your goals, why you're taking climbing lessons. And if you have gear, or if Eddie supplied you with what you need."

Gina shoved her mittened hands in her pockets and shuffled the few steps back to Dorje's truck, glad to cooperate. "Mountain High came highly recommended, and I've been dying to try ice climbing since moving here last year. A friend is visiting over spring break, and I plan to go climbing with him."

Dorje made a noise, almost a growl, then asked, "Is your friend a proficient climber?"

"Adventure Ted—" She began, instantly regretting that she'd shared Ted's preferred name. Should she worry that her friend's choice of monikers made her embarrassed for him?

"Adventure what? Is that really his name?" She didn't have to see Dorje's face to know he'd raised his eyebrows.

"It's what people call him. And I don't know what his skill level is, but I'm sure he has lots of experience."

Another rumble came from Dorje, low, almost unperceivable, but slightly judgmental. "We'll make sure you're as prepared as possible."

"Sounds good to me," she agreed with a smile. "Should we walk down to the ice?" Why hang around the truck talking when she could be building those skills?

She'd already turned again to collect her pack when he responded, "Yeah, no."

"But I have gear. You saw it yesterday. I borrowed some from Mari. I think you know her."

"She's a friend," he intoned.

"She said to say hi."

He hesitated, big, gloved fists clenching. "Did she say anything else? Uh, about me?"

He acted cagey, like Mari had been when they'd first discussed Dorje. What were they hinting at? "Well, yeah. She said you were one of the best and that I was lucky to be scheduled with you."

"Oh." Dorje gave a slow nod. "Uh, that was nice of her. Mari was great with Nana, my grandmother, at the retirement center."

"Mari mentioned her too. I'm sorry for your loss."

He dipped his head. "Thank you. She passed in her sleep over a year ago."

Gina thought back to Mari's comments. Had his year been rough because of his grandmother's death?

After a moment, Dorje rubbed his gloved hands together and changed the subject. "Ready for today's lesson?"

Gina bounced on her toes. "I was born ready." She'd nearly shouted in her enthusiasm and had to check herself, reel it in.

"I've got something for you," Dorje said as he unzipped the breast pocket of his jacket and pulled out a small, laminated card—on his third try. It looked like a difficult task with gloves on, but he didn't take them off. Printed on the card was Mountain High's list of ten essentials for outdoor adventures.

"You might have seen these before in various forms," he said. He took a wide stance, his covered hands clasped in front of him like he lectured to a room full of students, not one woman in a snowy pullout. "But I can't stress enough how important they are. Keep the list with you. Refer to it often. Don't become complacent."

Gina looked up at her instructor. She might not have been able to see his eyes, but they pinned her to the spot, nonetheless. "Is this because of yesterday?"

He shook his head. "I start every lesson this way. The items on the list might save your life. We'll go over each one."

Her eyes grew wide. "Right now?"

"This is part of your first lesson."

"Standing here in the cold?"

"Do you know what a belay is?"

She blinked at his apparent change of topic. "I assume it's the same as at the rock gym. When you're belaying, you're anchoring the person climbing."

He nodded. "And when you're ice climbing, it means that you're standing in the cold, not moving much, while your partner climbs."

Right. Lessons. She grimaced, then read from her

card, "Essential number two. Dress in layers, bring extra clothes. Okay," she conceded as the cold crept into her open collar. She zipped it shut. "Point taken. Should we start from the top?"

Gina couldn't pinpoint the change in Dorje, but she liked to think she'd made him smile. "Number one," he said, apparently reciting from memory. "Navigation. Phones are great until they aren't. You can lose cell coverage or your batteries can die in the cold. Have a backup, know how to read a map and use a compass. Many ice climbs aren't this close to the road. You'll need to find your way to the ice and, more importantly, back to your car."

Gina leaned on the truck as Dorje continued down the list, going over headlamps, first aid, multi-tools, fire, food, hydration, and shelters. He might have sounded a bit like a professor, but he had her full attention. These were important details.

He turned his face, concealed behind fabric and blue-tinted ski goggles, up to the sky as he hit the last item on the list—the sun. "With the short days during the Alaska winter, it might not seem like an important one, but flat light can make visibility hard. And once the sun is higher in the sky, you don't want to be without a quality pair of sunglasses."

"And sunscreen," Gina added, instantly regretting her comment, especially when Dorje didn't respond immediately. *Good going, Gina. Bringing up skin protection with the guy who is sensitive about his skin.*

After a moment, he bobbed his head. "Yes, right. That's very important too."

"This is also for you," he said as he lifted a clear, liter-sized water bottle out of the back of his truck and handed it to her. "Safety gear. It contains an emergency blanket, knife, matches, and a small first-aid kit."

Gina shook the bottle to see all the goods. "Excellent, thanks," she said, pausing a nanosecond before asking, "Now can we play on the ice?" She cringed at the pleading tone of her voice. Like an eager kid asking for dessert. She rocked on her feet. Her body and mind were ready to ice climb the right way.

Dorje remained silent a moment, and she thought he might say no. "Our safety lesson isn't over," he stressed, "but we can go down to the falls."

Before she could think better of it, Gina gave in to impulse and jumped forward, wrapping her arms around her massive instructor. "Yeeessss!" she cried.

GINA HAD CAUGHT Dorje by surprise. He stood with his arms raised, looking down at her wrapped around his middle. It was hard—no, impossible—to be stern with this charismatic woman who didn't seem capable of standing still, her excitement to walk down to the falls too great.

Her touch sent a flash of awareness through him, but before he could reciprocate and put an arm around her, she released him and bounded back a few steps. Her freckled cheeks were rosy from standing in the cold, but they'd taken on a deeper color, and she quickly glanced away as if avoiding eye contact.

Was she embarrassed because she'd spontaneously hugged her instructor, or had she also felt a spark when her arms encircled his body?

She took a step toward her car and stopped, turning to him. "Now can I get my backpack?"

He nodded. "Yeah, but don't think you're immediately going to scale that waterfall. First, we go over gear and more safety."

She cracked a wide smile. "Got it."

Gina returned with her bag while Dorje finished packing his backpack. She was fast, eager, and stood there watching him as he strapped a last sling of ice screws to the side of his bag—not that they'd need them today. They clanged together as he shouldered the load.

Gina's hand feathered over the pieces of protection. "Am I going to learn about these?"

He grunted. "Eventually." Then he raised an arm toward the trail. "After you. I think you know the way."

She tossed him a good-natured smirk before taking off down the trail, remarking on the birdsong, the glittering snow in the weak rays of sun, and the color of the winter sky. She stopped suddenly, eyes closed, and breathed in. "It's so beautiful here," she remarked. "I love how fresh the air is."

"Mmm," he agreed. Yes, beauty surrounded them, but he only had eyes for Gina that morning. She was cute when she bounced around and stunning when she stopped and closed her eyes. He resisted the impulse to tear off his face cover and goggles, to breathe in deeply and feel the cold air against his own skin.

When she opened her eyes, her smile appeared serene. Like she'd just connected herself to nature, to her surroundings.

"How long have you lived here?" she asked as they continued down the trail.

"Born and raised."

"Oh, right. Your grandma lived here too."

"She raised me. My family goes way back in the region." He didn't elaborate and changed the subject before Gina asked questions he couldn't answer, not if he wanted to keep yeti a secret.

They'd reached the downed cottonwood tree at the base of the falls. Dorje took off his pack. "First, we put our crampons on before we step out onto the ice."

Gina sat next to him on the log. "For the record, I didn't go out on the creek ice yesterday without them. I even punctured my cuff while wrestling them on."

Dorje raised a booted foot to show her the hem of his snow pants. "This is usually the most common location for snags." He'd torn his in a couple of places where he'd caught the sharp metal tips while walking.

They both strapped on their crampons, and then Dorje led Gina down the creek, away from the falls. "It's good to experience walking over different angles of ice." The uneven terrain included bare ice and patches of snow.

When the creek passed over a series of boulders at a low angle, Dorje turned, and they walked back. Gina appeared well-balanced on the spikes. She didn't need more practice—at least not simply walking with crampons on.

"Your next challenge," Dorje said, as they returned to the log, "is to put on your climbing harness."

Gina looked down at the metal spikes on her feet. "Can I take these off first?"

He shook his head.

"Why do I get the impression that you have an evil grin under that face mask?" she asked.

She believed he'd make her put her boots and crampons through the leg loop. That made him smile. But Mari would kill him if he allowed Gina to shred her loaned equipment. "The leg loops on your harness are adjustable and can be fully opened." He stepped over to show her. "Here," he said, tugging the strap through one of the leg loop buckles, "this opens it up. Do the same on the other side and at the waist."

Gina took off her gloves to work the straps. Dorje didn't have the luxury, not if he wanted to keep his blue hands covered.

Once she had her harness open, he demonstrated with his own. "Start with the waistband. We'll adjust the fit once you have everything on."

Gina mimicked his actions, working the buckle at her stomach, then her legs.

"May I?" he asked, gesturing to her harness waistband. "In the beginning, I'd like to check the buckles to ensure they're tight. After you get the hang of it, we can do a verbal check-in with one another. It's a safety precaution—make sure you don't become so busy gabbing with a friend at the pitch that you forget to double back your straps before clipping in."

Gina lifted her arms, her focus on the harness. "Yeah, of course." Then she laughed when he moved from her waistband to her leg straps along her inner thigh. "I see why you asked permission. You're all up in my business."

He tugged at one leg strap, then reached between her legs for the other buckle. "But I'm all business about it." He snugged that strap as well. These weren't caresses, but yeah, he'd just buried his hand between Gina's legs. A flash of heat pulsed through him when he thought of it that way. *Do not think sexy thoughts about your client!*

He quickly moved back to her middle, placed his hands on either side of her harness, and tugged on the waistband. "Good," he said when he met resistance.

"It won't slide over your hips. If you can wiggle a hand through the strap, it should be perfect. Not too loose, not too tight." Dorje realized he still had his hands on Gina's hips as he spoke. He quickly dropped them and took a big step back while she tried it.

"I've heard that for rock climbing harnesses too," she admitted, but huffed a laugh. "It's a little harder to fit a hand through the strap with all these winter clothing layers."

"No doubt." Unlike some yeti, Dorje had worn clothes most of his life and couldn't imagine climbing without them. But he had wondered what it would be like to venture outdoors without tech gear. After all, he had a natural build for it.

"Is it time to rope up?" Gina asked, her tone hopeful.

He might be cruel, but Dorje had no intention of roping up today—he hadn't even packed a rope. No climbing during the safety and gear introduction session. He handed Gina her ice axes. "Let's practice swinging. You did a great job yesterday, but I'd like to give you some instruction and go over different methods."

Dorje ran through personal safety and several techniques for using the ice axe.

Gina learned quickly—though yesterday had more than proven that.

After she'd run through several exercises on both her right and left arms, he explained, "Climbers used to loop their wrists through a leash—a ring of webbing connected to the handle of an ice axe. But many have moved to using a tether."

"Ah . . . I'd wondered about that yesterday. Seems like I could have easily dropped an axe at any point."

He nodded and gestured to the ring of webbing at the front of her harness. "These connect to your belay loop. Because you weren't wearing a harness yesterday, you couldn't tether your ice axes."

"Huh. So, one more risk I should have avoided?"

He tipped his head in silent agreement.

Gina frowned, but seemed to shake it off immediately. "Well, I'm ready to tether and rope up today," she said cheerfully.

"We're not roping up today," he said and then teased, "Maybe tomorrow." He'd let her climb tomorrow, but wanted to see her reaction if she thought she couldn't.

"What?" She gestured to her middle and the tools at her feet. "I've got a harness on. We practiced swinging axes. You won't let me climb today, and tomorrow is a maybe?"

"We'll see how it goes," he said in a light voice. Too bad she couldn't see his playful smile.

She gave his arm a good-humored swat. "You are a tease."

Dorje's head tipped back with the force of his laugh. It took him by complete surprise. When had he last laughed? He couldn't remember. Tears sprung from his eyes, and his whole body felt loose and relaxed when he got himself under control. "You want to get your feet off the ground?" he asked in a rumbling voice.

Gina watched him, a curious smile on her face. Her brows dipped. "Yes," she said, hesitantly. "But why do I get a feeling this is a trick?"

Though she couldn't see his eyes, he held her gaze while he reached down and curled his hand through her belay loop. "We can simulate climbing," he said before he lifted her into the air.

Gina squealed a laugh and grabbed his arm to balance herself as her feet came up off the ground. "Holy shit, I cannot believe you just did that." She looked down. "Actually, I can't believe that anyone can do this." Her hand slowly slid around his upper arm, and her tongue darted out to lick her lips. "Just how big is your bicep?"

Her heated gaze traveled down his arm to his hand, which was mere inches from the juncture of her legs.

"Big enough," he growled, not caring about the inappropriateness of this interaction between instructor and paying client.

Her smile widened as her gaze flicked back to his covered face. "That sounded dirty, Dorje."

Heat pulsed through him again.

In a teasing voice, she continued, "Withholding climbing and now this. And to think I brought you yarn today. I may not give it to you."

He blinked. She'd brought yarn for him? He slowly lowered her, his mind shifting from the electricity between them to the knit-a-thon. "Yarn?" Her feet met the ground, and he released her belay loop.

"Eddie mentioned you were looking for donations, and Mari told me you were knitting for charity. I tried knitting, thought it would be a great hobby for wintry days. But I made knots, not stitches. I have a couple of skeins for you. I'd love it if you can put them to good use."

"T-thank you," he said. "I appreciate that."

Gina smirked and crossed her arms. "Not so fast,

muscleman. You can have the yarn if I can rope up and climb tomorrow. Deal?"

He would have let her climb tomorrow, regardless. She was ready, and she'd paid for climbing lessons, not a multi-day safety course. "Deal." He held out his gloved hand, and she gave it a firm pump, her bright smile wide.

While Gina's actions had triggered him yesterday, her smile had the opposite effect. Dorje had undertaken these lessons out of desperation. He'd committed to producing knitted goods, plus the activity soothed his mind . . . but so did hanging out with Gina. His time with her would soon end, but until then, he'd enjoy every moment.

# CHAPTER FIVE

Gina had signed up for climbing lessons to impress a guy, not meet a new one. She'd let Ted believe she knew her way around an ice axe. She'd been attracted to him and wanted to bond over their shared interest. Flirting with her instructor or dreaming about his giant body pressed against hers hadn't been in her plans. And yet both had happened.

Gina and Ted weren't romantically involved, nor had they made any promises. Had she hoped they'd hook up while he was in town? Sure. But that desire was fading faster than a burned-out star. She still looked forward to her friend's visit. However, her growing attraction to Dorje was unlike anything she'd ever experienced. She'd never even seen his face, yet Gina was crushing hard.

A flush swept over her body at the memory of Dorje lifting her by her harness. He'd suspended her in the air by one arm—such a hot move. Wasn't there a saying about the size of a guy's bicep? His hand was so large that when wrapped around her belay loop, his gloved knuckles created a sweet, light pressure against her lower abdomen. So close to the good stuff, yet far enough away that it hadn't crossed a line. Although if she were honest, she would welcome some line-crossing from Dorje. The thought of it made her panties damp.

Gina forced a slow breath to clear her head. She had another lesson in thirty short minutes. She did not want to show up looking twitterpated and turned on, but she intended to accessorize for the occasion. Climbing Lower Fireweed Falls was a glitter-worthy event. Gina opened her container of multicolor body glitter and applied a dab to each cheek.

Would a little shimmer make Dorje scowl? Who knew what he hid under that face mask? But she had a hunch that deep down, he'd like it. She spread another line of sparkles up her cheekbone for good measure.

Dorje beat her to the parking area again. Her

belly fluttered at the sight of him, and she couldn't stop her grin. She waved as she pulled in beside his truck. His tailgate wasn't down, no spread of gear for demonstration. A good sign.

Today, he wore the same jacket but sported a new light blue face mask tucked under his goggles. Maybe he'd arrived early to cover up before she got there. Yesterday, he'd pulled out behind her, but not close enough that she'd been able to see him in her rear-view mirror. Did he drive with the goggles on? Surely not.

Instead of grabbing her pack and assuming they were heading straight to the falls, Gina jogged around her car to say hello first. "Morning!"

"Good mor—" He stopped mid-word and gave her a double take.

Once again, she could only see her reflection—a satisfied smile—in his goggles.

He pointed a gloved finger at his own cheek. "You're . . . shiny."

"Yep. I'm climbing a waterfall today."

He grunted, and she translated it to: "I'm confused about my feelings, but I like you and your sparkling face."

"I brought some for you to wear as well. We can put it on your goggles."

He leaned back as she stepped forward with the jar of glitter in hand. His back hit the truck. "You want to put glitter on me?"

She nodded, a smear of the shiny stuff on her outstretched finger. She closed in on him in the tight space between the open door and the inside of his truck.

A sigh of resignation seemed to flutter Dorje's face mask as he bent his knees, lowering himself to her level. Gina carefully placed a glittery streak on the frames and not the lenses. "There," she said, admiring her work—and searching in vain for a glimpse of Dorje's eyes through the goggles. She might have seen an eyelash flutter, but nothing more.

She pulled out her phone. "Can I take a selfie of us?"

"You want me in your picture?"

She playfully nudged him with her shoulder. "Heck yeah."

"Just don't post it online."

She agreed and snapped several shots. Dorje might have covered up and been private, but he hammed it up for selfies. He gave the sign of the horns in one and wrapped his arm around her in another. She'd be studying that one later.

Dorje moved to grab his pack. "We'd better get you up that ice."

Gina bounced on her feet, then dashed back to her car for her backpack. "I'm *so* ready."

When they arrived at the base of the falls, Dorje pointed to two lengths of bright purple rope lying against the ice. "Since we can access the top of the climb by foot, I built a top rope anchor before you arrived. Next week, I'll teach you how to do that."

Gina agreed to the plan, glad to focus today on the belay device, working with ropes and ice axes, and, finally, climbing.

They ran through Dorje's safety checks, which included him physically grabbing her harness again. Truly, she'd be sad when they moved to a verbal check, and he stopped manhandling the gear in her nether regions with his giant paws. He gave her an all-clear and explained climber dialogue.

"It's like rock climbing," he began. "When you're ready to start, call back to your belayer and ask, 'On belay?' As your belayer, I'll take in the slack on the rope and say, 'Belay on.' You follow with, 'Climbing,' and I'll say, 'Climb on,' letting you know I'm ready for you to start."

Gina ran through the dialogue with Dorje, and the taut rope pulled at her harness when he took up the slack. Then she was back on the ice, swinging the axes, digging in her toes. This time she had to watch out for the rope, but when she kicked in and lost her footing, she didn't slide. The harness and rope held her in place until she got a solid toe hold.

Being right-handed, Gina's left arm tired faster. By the time she neared the top, her left arm swings weren't as solid as those with her right arm, but otherwise, she felt great.

Per Dorje's instruction, she stopped below the top. It wasn't safe to climb up to or beyond the top rope anchor. "I did it," she cried, as she reached her highest position yet on the falls. The rope tugged on her harness as Dorje snugged in the remaining slack.

"Of course you did," he called from below.

Her body shook slightly with the sustained effort. All muscles were firing to hold herself in place. "So now I have to downclimb?" That wouldn't be easy—though at least this time, there wouldn't be dire consequences if she slipped.

"Nope, I'll lower you. Sit back in the harness."

Gina peered down at Dorje. "Sit?" Was he out of his mind?

"Remember when you slipped going up and the harness caught you? This is the same idea, but you're controlling it."

When she remained silent, Dorje's deep, confident voice traveled up the falls. "The rope is solid, the knots tight. We checked your harness. I've got you, Gina. Trust the system, trust yourself, trust me."

She did trust Dorje—even if she'd never seen his face. Gina let out a breath as she eased back, testing her weight on the rope and harness. It held. She transferred the rest of her weight until she sat in the harness facing the ice, shaky arms now at her sides.

"How you doing?" Dorje asked. "Is the view nice?"

The view. She'd forgotten to look. Carefully, she made a half-turn, not fully comfortable with her position. "Everything looks amazing from the top of a waterfall."

"No doubt," Dorje replied. She'd swear there was a smile in his voice. "Ready to come down? Put your feet out in front of you and 'walk' down the ice as I lower you."

Gina did as he instructed and descended to the base in seconds. "Coming down was fun!"

As soon as she untied from the rope, she threw her arms around Dorje. They only wrapped around a portion of his massive form, but she couldn't stop herself. She was a hugger, and he'd helped her accomplish a goal. "Thank you," she cried.

The cherry on top of her accomplishment? Dorje's arms slowly slid around her back and locked her in place. "Good job, Gina," he rumbled, the vibrations passing from his body into hers where they pressed together. She never wanted to let go.

Gina had met two goals. One she'd planned for—climbing Lower Fireweed Falls. And one she hadn't—coaxing a return hug from Dorje, his cedar and vanilla scent curling around her. Could she accomplish both goals at every climbing lesson?

She bit her lip to hide a smile. Gina *never* shied away from a challenge.

<hr />

DORJE HAD no problem doling out high fives and hugs for client achievements. Embraces generally fell into two categories: the bro half-hug, more of a clap on the back, or the quick clench from someone pumped full of adrenaline and excitement.

Hugging Gina didn't fit into either of Dorje's established categories. But how did *she* categorize it? Should he care? Should he even still be thinking about it more than an hour later while he lowered the woman down from her third climb? Definitely not.

"Got another one left in you?" Dorje half-teased as Gina's boots hit the ground. Even with glittery cheeks and an unwavering smile, she looked spent.

She wistfully glanced up at the ice and shook her head. "I don't think so. I'm ready for a break." She untied from her harness. "But what about you? Do you want to climb?" She clasped her forehead. "I should have asked earlier. My arms are as floppy as overcooked asparagus."

Narrowing her eyes, she took him in from head to toe. He fought the urge to puff out his chest. He squared his shoulders instead.

She asked, "Am I big enough to belay you? How would that work?"

"You *could* belay me," Dorje explained, "but we'd need to anchor you to a cottonwood tree. Otherwise, if I fell while you were on belay, I might launch you into the air."

Gina chuckled. "I don't want to drop you or go airborne."

"I'll show you belaying another time," he said, loving how her eyes brightened at the suggestion of learning something new. Or was she looking forward to their next time together? He'd like to think it was both. After seeing Gina three days in a row, he would miss her over the weekend. It would be four long days before their next lesson the following Tuesday.

Dorje showed Gina how to coil the rope and she carried it the short distance to the log where they'd left their packs. "I brought something for you," he added as they sat on the log. He pulled a zip-top bag from his backpack. "Chocolate chip cookies as a thank you for the yarn and to celebrate your first ice climb."

Gina immediately opened the bag and pulled one out. "Oh my god," she said, around a large bite. "My favorite." She made a "mmm" sound. "These taste homemade. Did you make them?"

As Dorje nodded yes, Gina turned away from him and spit into her hand. "So good," she said, then turned and spit again, dark lumps collecting in her palm like watermelon seeds. "Thank you."

He shook his head. "If you like them, then what are you spitting out?"

Her eyes grew wide, and she swallowed. "Chocolate chip cookies are my favorite, but I don't like the chocolate chips. But the rest of the cookie . . ." She trailed off, rolling her eyes in pleasure. She took a bite while giving him an enthusiastic thumbs up.

"So next time I make cookies for you, leave out the chocolate chips?"

She gave him the side eye, her glittery cheeks rounded with a grin. "You're going to make cookies for me again?"

Well, crap. He'd said that as if it was a foregone conclusion. "I, uh . . ." He stumbled over his words.

Before the climbing accident last year, he'd baked regularly. He and Nana had baked together when he was young, his half-brother Yeshe helping when he was in town. He'd enjoyed baking again last night. Maybe because he'd thought of Gina the whole time. Ugh. Whatever. His infatuation would pass when the lessons were over. At that point, Gina would be hanging out with *Adventure Ted*.

Gina took pity on him. "My mom separates the dough and only adds chocolate chips to half."

"So, you don't like chocolate?" he clarified.

"I love chocolate. But I like chocolate chip cookies best without the chocolate chips."

Dorje closed his eyes, his brain struggling to find logic. "That doesn't make sense."

"Let me put it this way. What would you call a chocolate chip cookie without chocolate chips?"

"A . . . sugar cookie?"

"But it isn't really a sugar cookie," she argued. And she was right.

"Okay, fair. The next time I make you cookies, they'll be chocolate chipless."

He half expected another hug and was oddly disappointed when all he got was a shoulder nudge. This woman had done a number on him.

They sat in silence for a moment. Awkward. He couldn't eat or drink in front of her without spilling his secret. He hadn't thought of that when he handed over the cookies.

Gina pulled him out of his thoughts. "When I was at the top of the falls, there was a little indentation, like a small cave."

He knew the location. "It's where the water passes over a large boulder. It's not big enough to climb into though. Not like the ice cave at Fireweed Glacier."

Gina's features froze. "There's an ice cave at the glacier?"

Shoot. Now he'd done it. She had a gleam in her eye like she was already picturing herself on a new adventure. "Yeah, but don't go exploring it in summer without a knowledgeable local. It can flood. Glaciers are unpredictable that way." From what he knew of Gina, she'd want to trek into the depths of a cave like that.

"It's winter now," she said, her eyes still on him.

*Ah, shit. She wants me to go with her.*

"Mari is always busy when I'm free. Adven . . . uh, Ted doesn't arrive for another week. I've done a few events with the trail running group in town. But I don't really know anyone, and I've been hesitant to go to the glacier by myself in winter."

"Don't go alone," he blurted, then tried again, figuring she wouldn't take that demand well. "You can go alone. Just be smart about it and tell someone where you're going."

Gina nodded. "Dorje, I'm going to the ice cave tomorrow. I'll leave at nine o'clock—earlier if it's light enough. I'll be back . . ." She paused. "How long does it take to hike there? And can you tell me where it is? You can drop me the coordinates."

Drop her the coordinates? He almost laughed. He could probably figure out how to do that, but he knew the terrain so well, it seemed unnecessary—to him, anyway. But they would be crucial for Gina. And he really didn't want her going there by herself. *She wouldn't be by herself if I went with her.*

He'd like to think that the voice in his head focused on safety first. It didn't. The loudest voice was the one angling for Gina to wrap her arms around him again.

"I'm free tomorrow and can go with you. If you

want my company." A giant beast with no exposed fur.

"Are you kidding?" Gina's eyes practically bulged from her face. She jumped up, as if unable to contain her excitement. "I'd love it if you came with me."

And then? Dorje got another hug. A quick one that he couldn't respond to. But her arms were on his person. Plus, their time apart just got cut down by a day, and he now had a hiking date with Gina. He already knew she'd love Fireweed Ice Cave, which made him ridiculously happy.

## CHAPTER SIX

The next morning, Gina didn't need caffeine to kick-start her day. She was buzzing from the exhilaration of successfully climbing a frozen waterfall—three times—and her planned hike with Dorje.

She'd done it. Legit climbed ice. And today she'd explore a glacial ice cave with a hot, faceless, seven-foot man who'd made cookies for her. Who wouldn't find that exciting? With Dorje's help, she was developing a skill set and gaining experience. These would empower her to engage in outdoor activities safely with others—like Ted . . . She hadn't thought much about her friend, not when she had a day with Dorje to look forward to.

When Gina arrived at the trailhead, Dorje was sitting on a wooden post next to an interpretive sign about glacial valleys. No truck, only the hulking man in his familiar outdoor gear and a mid-sized backpack for a day hike.

After exchanging greetings, she said, "Don't tell me you hiked to the trailhead."

His face mask moved as if he smiled. "Okay, I won't tell you that," he deadpanned. Dorje then pulled his backpack around and unzipped it. "Brought something for you." He handed Gina another bag of cookies.

She turned it in her hands. No dark lumps.

He'd baked for her.

Again.

And these cookies were perfect. No chocolate chips.

It meant he'd been thinking about her last night. God, he made her feel special. Was he just being nice, or did he feel an attraction too? When he made her cookies, was he thinking about lifting her by her harness? *I have to get that out of my mind!* She never would. When she turned ninety, she'd still remember feeling weightless while he held her by thin straps around her girly bits.

Gina tried to clear those thoughts as she pushed up on her toes to plant a quick, chaste kiss against Dorje's covered face. She'd never have been able to reach if he weren't sitting on the post. "You're too sweet, Dorje. Thank you."

"I baked for the retirement center. And I did as you instructed, separating some of the dough before adding the chocolate chips. I made what you like: dull, boring cookies. For someone who celebrates with glitter, I thought you'd want to replace the chocolate with something like confetti sprinkles."

Gina's lips twitched, and her heart raced around in her chest. He was cute, clever, and thoughtful. She arched a brow. "We aren't always what other people expect, are we?"

Dorje went curiously still. "What did you mean by that?"

She waved a hand, trying to put him at ease. "Nothing. Just that sometimes we're more than what we appear." But he seemed to read her like a book. Confetti sprinkles would be awesome.

Adjusting their packs, they started down the trail. The first part of the hike followed the narrow Fireweed Canyon. "This section," Dorje said, pointing up at the rock walls, "can be prone to avalanches under certain conditions. And in summer, it can flood. Always check the forecasts before coming out here. The snowpack is stable today, though."

The valley opened into a classic, wide U-shape, typical of glacial erosion. Gina had only become familiar with this type of landscape since moving to Wildwood. Steep, rocky walls lined a nearly flat, miles-wide valley floor that gently sloped up to the present-day glacier face.

Dorje chatted about the glacier, the valley, and the seemingly endless recreational activities. For someone who didn't want to show his face, he had no problem making conversation, at least not with her.

They eventually came to a fork in the snowy trail near the glacier's face. Most of the foot and ski traffic had turned right. "The route to the right leads to a place where it's easy to climb onto the glacier. Trails branch from there, like access to Little Bear Valley. But we're going left," he explained. A lone set of old ski tracks marked the way.

Gina couldn't help but smile. "We're taking the path less traveled."

"It makes all the difference," Dorje quipped ahead of her. It looked like he purposefully took short steps as he stomped down the fresh snow, making it easier for Gina to follow.

Although it still thrilled her to be so close to a glacier, it was anticlimactic this time of year. Except for some crevasses higher in the glacier that shone blue-green, snow covered the mass of ice, making it look no different than the valley floor.

The glacier's terminus spanned more than a mile across. Gina followed Dorje as they paralleled the face to the west. "How often do you come out here?" she asked. "Does Mountain High offer tours?"

Dorje's step faltered. "No, no tours. Most people who know about the cave don't share the information." His big shoulders shrugged. "It would be a shame if it became everyone's weekend destination. Plus, these things come and go as the glacier changes. This one has been around for years, but it won't last forever."

Gina glanced back at their footprints in the snow. "But everyone will see our tracks."

"The wind often howls through here." It *had* picked up. Some of their marks were already drifting in. "The forecast calls for snow tomorrow." He turned back to her as if smiling. "No one will ever know."

That could have sounded creepy, but it wasn't. It felt like a shared secret. Something special between them. She tucked her chin into her jacket collar to hide her pleased grin.

Eventually, they rounded a corner, and the dark opening of the large ice cave lay before them. With its wavy blue-green walls, it looked like it had been carved out of a frozen ocean wave.

Dorje led her into the cavern until the magic surrounded them. The twenty-foot-tall opening narrowed to about ten feet as they rounded a corner. Sound became muted, making her more aware of her loud breathing and pounding heart. The dimpled aquamarine walls and ceiling surrounded them—like being inside a gemstone. Breathtaking.

Dorje had said he didn't take clients here. Locals didn't share it with outsiders. For the first time since moving to Alaska, Gina finally felt like she belonged. He'd let her in, made her feel welcome. Her chest swelled with a sense of belonging.

He stood at her shoulder, a silent companion letting her take it all in. But she needed more, craved a connection. Gina held her breath and slowly reached the few inches for Dorje's gloved hand. At worst, he'd brush her off. At best, he'd hold her hand. But she'd never know until she tried.

FIREWEED Ice Cave was a special place for Dorje. After the accident, he didn't want to trek across glaciers or climb mountains, but he had no problem visiting this place. He'd come here more than once just to be present. Some people might call it meditation. Dorje found peace here.

And now he shared it with a complex woman who preferred flavorless cookies but who otherwise bubbled over with color and cheerfulness. A woman who . . . had slipped her hand into his.

He tried not to look down at her small green mitten in the palm of his large black glove. This wasn't a casual brush—she gave his hand a light squeeze and didn't let go.

*What am I getting myself into?* He'd known better than to agree to this hike. It changed their relationship from instructor and client to friends. But Dorje couldn't be Gina's true friend. She didn't know about yeti, and he couldn't tell her. Today was the one and only time they'd be together outside of a climbing lesson.

He stifled a groan and tightened his grip on her hand. If this was his only chance, he wouldn't waste the opportunity to share something special and intimate with Gina.

"Incredible," she whispered as, hand-in-hand, they turned a slow circle. She peered into the deep, dark blue at the back of the cave. "How far does it go?"

"A ways farther," he said, tugging on her hand and turning on his headlamp as he led her deeper into the cave. They stopped at a point where the ice narrowed, and they'd have to drop to their hands and knees if they went farther. "I crawled back there a couple of years ago, but it's inaccessible now after shifting ice."

Gina's hand tightened in his, her gaze moving to the low, icy ceiling. "Should I be worried?"

He shook his head. "Glaciers move slowly, and most of the dynamic action happens at the height of summer thaw. We're safe." He probably sounded like a broken record. If Gina learned anything from him, he hoped it included safety awareness.

They made their way back towards the opening. Gina rested on a large rock in the center of the cave and snacked, while Dorje played with the various modes of his headlamp, lighting up the ice. He had to busy himself with something while she ate. She needed the fuel, and he needed to keep his face covered.

"So, you're a math teacher?" Dorje asked then inwardly winced. He basically had to ghost Gina when her lessons were over, so he shouldn't ask personal questions. But he couldn't help himself. He wanted to know her better.

"Tutor," she corrected.

"What's the difference?" Eyebrows raised, she gave him a surprised look. Should he have known? "My grandmother homeschooled me," he explained.

"I help students with one subject, usually math, outside of school. We focus in-depth on specific topics." She told him about her students, who lived all over the country.

As they exited the cave, he shared things he wouldn't normally share, like his online knitting community that related to her widespread group of students. The words kept flowing. Conversation with Gina was easy.

Snow fell as they reentered Fireweed Canyon. Gina quizzed him on his favorite color, food, and song. Fireweed purple, Nana's butter tea—not a food, per Gina. And no answer.

"Come on, you must like something. Eighties rock? Nineties alternative? Country? R&B? Several local bands play at the Wildwood Brewery. What about them?"

Dorje had never set foot in the part of the brewery where bands played. Though he had heard the music from the private events room where he, fellow yeti, and some yeti-friendly humans occasionally hung out.

A dusting of snow rained down on them from the slope above, saving him from explaining himself to Gina as he shifted his focus to her safety.

When pebbles followed the snow, Dorje grabbed Gina and ducked under an overhanging rock, prepared to cover her body with his own if more snow and rock slid down.

As the falling debris slowed, two shapes appeared across the narrow cut. "Damn mountain goats," Dorje mumbled. Although, honestly, they were cool—much nimbler than a yeti.

Gina didn't reply.

"Did you see them—" he said, stopping mid-sentence when heat from her bare palm warmed his cheek. His heart gave a slow, sluggish beat. Her hot hand moving up his cheek, and the bite of winter cold on his nose meant one thing. His neck gaiter had fallen, exposing his face.

Gina sat in his lap, cradled in his arms, while he perched on a slab of rock. Her eyes were not on the goats. They were on him. She stared into his goggles as if she could see his eyes. "Just what kind of skin condition do you have, Dorje?"

*Fuuuck!*

## CHAPTER SEVEN

D orje was watching the mountain goats, but Gina was watching him.

When he'd picked her up like she was no heavier than a box of bubble wrap and whisked her under the ledge, the neck gaiter he used as a face mask had fallen. She shifted in his lap to better see his face.

She blinked.

His *blue* face.

A trimmed, snowy-white beard lined a pronounced jaw, and whiskers pricked her palm when she cupped his cheek. Large canine teeth created slight indentations against lush and, well . . . kissable lips the color of deep-blue winter twilight.

Dorje's growl reverberated through her body, the

sensation pooling between her thighs. Possibly because she'd spread *her* legs wide to straddle *his* enormous legs. Her core throbbed in response to the vibration, the heat of his massive body seeping into hers, and his unique features that were suddenly on display.

"It's not a skin condition," he said, his voice hushed and raspy.

Her hands moved to his goggles. "I want to see you." She hesitated, desperate to study the rest of his face. But she wouldn't proceed without his permission. "Please?"

His hands covered hers. Gone were the giant black gloves. In their place were warm, blue fingers and white hair on his wrists that ghosted over her skin like a soft downy feather. She fought a shiver at the pleasurable sensation. Then he slowly helped her lift the goggles.

He whispered her name like a plea and a confession.

Gina took him in, continuing to explore with her eyes and hands.

Azure lips contrasted with lighter blue skin. It reminded her of the depths of the ice cave. His trim white beard led to longer, softer, white . . . fur? She swallowed. Yes, fur—along the side of his face, his head. She lightly rubbed at his temples, where it had matted under his goggles.

Eyes the color of an aquamarine gemstone stole her breath. The goats could have stampeded through the creek bed, and still she couldn't have torn her gaze away. Her smile grew. Then she giggled. "Dorje, you have some seriously big secrets, don't you?" She paused, then asked, "What are you?"

His chest rose and fell with a sigh. "A yeti."

"That's so badass."

"We, ah, need to talk."

"I'll say."

---

HOW HAD he let this happen?

Stupid question. Dorje knew exactly how he'd revealed himself, and the whole yeti race, to a new human. He'd taken a risk. Gotten too close. He liked Gina and her over-the-top enthusiasm, cheerful attitude, and ability to focus when needed—and he'd thrown caution to the wind. A bright spark in his gloomy world, she'd occupied most of his thoughts since meeting her.

She hadn't screamed and wasn't running. Instead, she straddled his legs while caressing his face with her fingertips. If she touched his lips again, he might lose control. An image of her *naked* and straddling him flashed through his mind.

Her thighs squeezed his legs as if in response to his daydream, and Dorje shot to his feet to stop his wayward thoughts. He was far too aware of Gina's snow pants sliding against his before her feet hit the ground. He bumped his head on the rocky overhang as he attempted to put space between them. "We'd better get back."

"And talk?"

"Yes. I need to explain things to you." He heaved a sigh. "This is a big secret that isn't only mine. It's imperative that you keep it."

Her eyes went wide. "There are other yeti?"

He tried not to roll his eyes and instead put himself in her tiny boots. "I had a mother and father."

She grimaced, her hand going to her forehead. "Right. And Nana." She slowly dropped her hand. "But she lived at the retirement center so she must have been human."

"She was," he confirmed as he led Gina out from under the ledge. A group of mountain goats scattered as they emerged.

Gina let out a "Wow," and reached for her phone to take a picture.

Dorje glared at the animals, wanting to blame them for his current predicament, but *he* was to blame. "Don't take any pictures of me, please." He hated he had to ask, but he couldn't risk it. Pictures could be accidentally posted online or seen by others.

They'd been back on the trail for several minutes when Gina called from behind. "Do you want to come over to my place," she asked, on a labored breath, "for dinner?"

Dorje hadn't realized how fast he'd been walking with his long, frustrated strides. Gina was jogging behind him to keep up. He stopped, and she nearly ran into him. "Sorry, I'll slow down."

She presented him with a dazzling smile. "It's fine. I love to run."

Of course she did.

Her smile grew even wider. "We should go out sometime together. I'll run. You can scowl and power-walk out your frustrations. We'd be about the same pace."

It didn't look like she was joking. "I'm not scowling," he shot back. Except he was, though. *Damn it!*

She patted his upper arm. "I've got soup in the slow cooker. Come over for dinner."

Dinner? Dorje paused, considering her offer. He'd had plenty of dinner invitations this past year. Tseten sometimes brought dinner over when Dorje refused to leave his house. But tonight, he actually wanted to accept. He'd spent all day with Gina, and it wasn't enough. His longing to be with her had nothing to do with telling her about yeti lore. No, he simply wanted her company, needed it like a healing balm. Being with her made him happy, and he hadn't felt that emotion in a long time.

"Okay," he said lamely. But then he couldn't resist teasing her. "But do you like your soup like you like your cookies? Will this be a pot of broth with nothing in it?"

She rewarded him with a grin that made his insides flutter. "Funny, Dorje. Very funny." She walked past him, then began jogging back to the trail-head. "You'll have to come over to find out."

He wanted to shout, "Now who's the tease," but kept his mouth shut and followed her perky ass up the trail. Guess he had a dinner date.

## CHAPTER EIGHT

After trying on everything in her closet, Gina settled on a casual flannel dress paired with leggings. She didn't want to overdo it—dinner with Dorje wasn't actually a date. But she also didn't want to underdo it because she did kind of consider it a date. It would be the first time they'd see each other without bulky winter gear.

Since Dorje's unexpected reveal a few hours earlier, the odd questions Mari had asked about him made more sense. Mari *knew* he was a yeti.

Gina had so many questions—and luckily, she'd soon have answers. Snow crunched in her driveway. She flipped her curtain back to watch Dorje's truck come to a stop. She let out a snicker. Now she'd finally learn if he wore goggles all the time.

No goggles, but he pulled up the hood of his black winter jacket and glanced toward the closest cabin. If her neighbors were looking, they'd be able to see him, but not well through the snow-covered trees.

Her heart began to race as he walked toward her door with a bottle in hand. Did wine mean this was a date? Hmm . . .

"Hi," she breathed as she ushered him in. "Did you find my place okay? The roads in this neighborhood are like a maze."

The corner of his mouth quirked up, lapis lips hitching in a partial smile beneath his snowy white beard. "I grew up here, remember? Can't get lost in Wildwood." He toed off his boots and hung his jacket by the door.

A beat passed as Dorje and Gina stood staring at each other. He wore a gray and brown plaid, button-up shirt—the type sold in sporting goods stores, though usually not in this size—tucked into canvas hiking pants. His socks matched the colors in his shirt. Rolled cuffs revealed thick, furry forearms. She knew the muscle that made those arms solid—he'd lifted her whole body with one of those arms, after all. Her stomach swooped at the memory. When her roaming gaze returned to his face, aquamarine eyes held hers and made her heart thump.

"Yeah, I wear normal human clothes," he said.

Heat flushed her cheeks, likely turning them a wild-rose pink, but she raised an eyebrow in challenge. "You were checking me out as well. Don't think I didn't notice."

He grunted in response, and she asked, "Don't all yeti wear clothes?" Since Dorje was the only yeti she'd met, she hadn't questioned that.

"Depends," was all he said.

It was on the tip of her tongue to tell him she now wondered what he looked like naked. But that might not be the best way to start their date—or whatever this was.

Dorje offered her the bottle he'd brought. "Do you drink wine? This is a red blend. Should pair well with broth."

She grinned at his joke and corrected him. "It's a family recipe called Brunswick Stew. I made it with chicken though, not squirrel or rabbit like my great-grandfather would have."

His eyes lit up. "I can get you rabbit, have some in my freezer from Yeshe, my half-brother. He's also a yeti," Dorje explained.

"I have a twin sister," Gina shared, then unhelpfully added, "Emma's not a yeti. Thanks for the offer. Maybe next time."

Gina poured glasses of wine and invited Dorje to sit on her small loveseat. She'd found it at the Wildwood Transfer Station reuse deck, an ingenious Alaskan system where people could drop off gently used items, and others could pick them up for free. It barely fit the two of them, but it had been a real score for her budget and her small living room.

She clinked her glass to his. "We should toast."

His white eyebrow rose. "To me spilling secrets?"

Gina fought a frown as disappointment washed over her. "You had no intention of telling me?"

He shook his head.

That stung, but Gina tried not to show it. After all, they'd only met a few days earlier. Odd, it seemed longer, like she'd always known Dorje.

He rubbed a giant hand across his face. "It's not as easy as me deciding to tell someone. It's not just my secret. There's a yeti community, and we rely on each other to stay under the radar."

She paused, considering. "I think I understand. But what's the risk?"

"Loss of privacy and security. There's a sizable 'monster' hunter population. Some want pictures, others want a pelt and a head to mount."

Gina shivered. "That's horrific."

"Then there's the government—U.S. and others

who would gleefully lock us in cages and experiment on us for the rest of our lives."

"That sounds like a terrible movie." She grimaced, but raised her glass to his again. "Can we toast our new friendship? Even if it wasn't your original intention?"

"Gina, I—" Dorje stopped mid-sentence and blinked. His hand was on her knee.

They both stared at it for a beat, her heart thudding as the warmth from his palm radiated through her legging. She liked his touch, wanted that giant blue hand on her body. This was way better than a hug with bulky jackets on. *Score!* But he snatched his hand back as if it had moved there without his permission.

"For the record, I like you," he said. "And I'm glad you know about me. But it's complicated. I'm complicated." With a big, gusty sigh, he clinked his glass to hers. "To us."

"To us," she repeated, then gulped an overly large sip of wine as the tingling from his touch spread from her knee to the rest of her body. "Now," she said, "tell me everything."

Complicated or not, she had it bad for the yeti.

"YOU'RE MY FIRST."

Dorje regretted his word choice as Gina's summer-green eyes widened to the size of twin full moons. He dropped his napkin next to his empty bowl. "I mean, you're the first human with whom I've shared the yeti secret."

She drained her wineglass and muttered an, "Oh."

"The stew was delicious, thank you. But maybe we should move back to the couch and I'll start from the beginning."

"Yes, let's," she said as she refilled their wine glasses before leading Dorje back to the living room. "And I'm glad you like my *broth*," she teased, using air quotes.

There'd been nothing dull about Gina's stew because, truly, there was nothing dull about Gina. Even her unique preference for plain cookies. Dinner had been delicious. The meal and her companionship satisfied him in a way that he hadn't experienced since Nana died.

It took them a moment to situate themselves. Dorje wedged himself in one corner of the couch, his body and legs rotated toward Gina. She tucked her legs under herself in the other corner. Her knees hit his thighs once she relaxed into place. He should have moved, put space between them. But he didn't.

"Where was I," he mused. "Oh yeah, yeti and humans are on the same family tree."

She giggled. "I didn't realize we were going that far back, but I'm with you. You mean like humans and Neanderthals?"

She'd asked one question, and he didn't know how to answer. "I guess? Sure. But we weren't absorbed into the human population like Neanderthals." He scratched his head and sipped his wine. "I guess what I'm getting at is that yeti and humans coexist, even if most humans aren't aware of it." He paused, then added, "And we interbreed."

He tried to say that last bit fast, as if he wasn't thinking about breeding with Gina. He imagined pushing her back into the couch, her legs wrapping around his waist, locking him in place against her small, firm body.

When she innocently asked, "Like your grandparents?" The erotic images immediately faded.

"Yes, Nana was human, and my grandfather was a yeti. Their relationship had ended before she realized she was carrying his child."

Gina sucked in a breath. "Single and pregnant with a *yeti's* baby . . ." She quickly covered her mouth to stop a giggle. "I don't mean to laugh, but that sounded like a tabloid headline. Your poor grandmother. What a difficult time that must have been for her."

"It was challenging," he agreed. "She had my mom, a yeti, and raised her here in Wildwood. Mom got pregnant after a one-night stand with another yeti. But she had itchy feet and left me with Nana while she traveled. She died in an avalanche in the Alps when I was young."

"Oh, Dorje," Gina exclaimed. "That's so sad."

He lifted a shoulder. "Yes and no. I don't have any memories of her. Not really. Shadows, you know. Memories that aren't real, just pictures I've seen of the two of us."

"So, Nana raised you?" Gina leaned forward to set her wineglass on the table. Her movement pressed more of her leg into his, and heat spread from the point of contact throughout his body. It was hard to stay focused on their conversation when his thoughts were on her touch.

"Yeah," he said. "At least by the time I came along, Nana had already raised one yeti. She said boy yeti were harder, especially when she oversaw two. My absent father had another son, Yeshe, my half-brother. Nana insisted Yeshe visit us often. He always came alone. I never met my father, which was fine. I only needed Nana."

Gina rested her elbow on the back of the couch, cradling her head as she gave him a thoughtful look. "Your relationship with your grandmother sounds like it was very special—enough that you stayed with her after you grew up."

A lump formed at the back of his throat at her words. Odd. Nana had been gone more than a year. He'd processed that grief well before the accident. "I didn't inherit my mother's wanderlust, at least not to the same degree. And Nana and I loved and looked out for each other."

"That's sweet, Dorje. I'm very sorry for your loss." Gina picked up her wineglass again and swirled the contents. After a moment, she asked, "So, who else is a yeti? Eddie?"

He laughed, not that Gina could know about Eddie. "He's human and looks like Thor from the comic books." Her eyebrows rose and a surprising pang of jealousy flared. "Eddie's taken, though he and Karma—also a yeti—won't admit it."

"I don't go for blondes," she assured him, dowsing the small spark of envy.

"What *do* you go for?" he couldn't help but ask.

She gave him a coy look. "That's evolving."

Dorje's heart made a little double beat, like it had tripped over its own feet. Was she referring to Adventure Ted? Or him? Maybe neither.

Gina drained her wine. "Tell me more."

"Like what?"

"What do you eat? Do you hunt? How do you buy groceries? Do you have a social security number? Do you ever go to the doctor? What does your fur feel like?" She narrowed her eyes as her gaze traveled up his torso. "I have a lot of questions."

Green eyes held his as he responded, "Tonight, I ate stew. I do hunt—with a hunting rifle, like humans. I have groceries delivered. A midwife saw to my social security number when I was born. She's the only medical professional most yeti around here ever see." Then he placed his arm, palm side up, in her lap. "This is what my fur feels like," he said, his voice low as he waited nervously for her reaction.

Gina traced his blue palm, her fingers whispering over his skin. She eased her way to the white fur on his wrist and forearm, the back of his hand. "You're so soft," she breathed.

A growl rumbled in his chest. "You mean manly?"

Her lips curved into a smile that made him feel special. "Your fingers have calluses. Is that better?"

It was. And then, he boldly asked, "What does *your* skin feel like?"

A flush of pink crept up her chest and neck. How far down did the blush continue? Would her breasts be the same gorgeous color?

Gina rested her palm in his. "I guess we have a lot to learn about each other."

Dorje curled his fingers around the smooth skin of Gina's hand. The air between them charged with electricity as he slowly brushed his thumb across the pulse point in her wrist.

But when he looked up, and their eyes met, a loud knock at the door broke the moment.

*Fuck!* Gina bolted to her feet, and Dorje mouthed that he'd be in her bathroom.

Dorje overheard, "Hey, sorry to bother you," before shutting himself into a room so tiny he barely managed to turn around.

But the knock had been a timely reality check. Gina had human friends and family that couldn't know about him.

As soon as her visitor left, he'd go home, back to his life. He shouldn't have been flirting with her tonight. Gina might know the yeti secret, but he needed to distance himself. He still had nightmares from the accident—he'd freaked out when she'd been climbing without a rope. He wasn't in a good head space. Plus, she had a friend—possibly a boyfriend—coming to town in a few weeks.

She might be the math tutor, but in his book, all this added up to a big fat negative.

## CHAPTER NINE

D orje's phone pinged again. He set down his knitting and paused his telenovela. He'd left Gina's place nearly twenty-four hours ago and had almost as many texts from her. Distancing himself was proving harder than he'd thought—at least while his phone was on.

All the texts started with "Do yeti . . .?" Everything from "Do all yeti wear socks?" to "Do yeti experience seasonal allergies?" She exhausted him, and he loved every minute of it.

> Gina: What are you doing tonight?

> Dorje: Collecting our text string to create a yeti Q&A.

> Gina: You're hilarious. But seriously, good idea.

Dorje smiled at his phone as three dots appeared. He could have gotten back to his knitting and show, but he didn't. He stared at his screen in anticipation of her next message.

> Gina: I've got to grade . . . If you're knitting, I could come over and grade while you knit. We can each do our thing but together. Also, you never responded to "Do all yeti live in caves?"

Dorje's heart began a slow hammer. Have Gina come to his home? Yes. He wanted that. His gut told him so. But his brain disagreed. Having Gina over would be like feeding a cute stray cat. Once fed, they were yours forever.

> Dorje: I don't live in a cave.

> Gina: Prove it.

> Dorje: A cave would have poor cell reception. I'm home now and texting you.

> Gina: I'm coming over. Don't turn the lights off and pretend you're not home. Also, bringing glitter.

Glitter. He snorted, but then pictured her naked body sparkling with the deuced stuff.

> Dorje: You don't know where I live.

> Gina: *devil face* Oh, but I do. And I have the code for your gate.

*Damn it.* He was going to kill Mari. He switched text strings.

> Dorje: You told Gina where I live and gave her the code?

> Mari: She has 4WD, can make it up your driveway. And she's good for you.

*What the fuck?*

> Dorje: Spinach is good for me.

He typed "Gina is . . ." but couldn't decide on the next word as he pictured her smile, her laughter. She embodied happiness.

> Mari: You made cookies, Dorj.
> Cookies—for her and us. You
> haven't baked since . . .

He knew exactly how long it had been. He hadn't made cookies since the accident. It had killed all his joy.

> Mari: . . . since Nana died. When
> you dropped off the cookies you
> looked so happy. You're baking and
> smiling again. *smiley face with
> hearts*

He'd made cookies since Nana had died. Hadn't he? Could he be wrong about the timing? He'd blamed the accident for plunging him into a funk that prevented him from finding pleasure in the things he'd previously enjoyed.

> Dorje: They're just cookies.

> Mari: *kissy smiley face* Open UR
> *blue heart*

What the fuck was that even supposed to mean? Dorje looked up from his phone. A car engine sounded in the distance.

Gina.

It would take her several minutes to navigate the

long, steep drive after she went through the gate. He jumped up, cleared several dishes off the counter, and put them in the sink. His gaze snagged on the kitchen table. Nana had kept a lace cloth under the fruit bowl, which unfortunately only contained a couple of browning bananas. He pulled the wrinkled fabric from a drawer and gave it a shake, then centered it under the dish.

The doorbell rang as he finished refolding a throw blanket and fluffing the pillows on the couch. He hit the button on the remote to kill his telenovela then pivoted to the door.

Gina wore a bright knit hat with a large, multi-color pom-pom. The pom-pom wasted a ton of yarn . . . Or did it? Maybe that was the perfect way to use up leftover scraps. Either way, it was very Gina. Fun, bright, and just a little extra.

She presented him with a dazzling smile. "I found you. Turns out," she said, looking around her, "that the one yeti I know lives in a badass house."

"With a killer view," he added. The house over-looked Fireweed Glacier. She'd love it. And he loved that she'd love it.

She was here now. He might as well enjoy himself. Dorje openly welcomed someone into his home for the first time in over a year. He hung Gina's jacket, then led her to the large picture window. "What do you think?"

Her gasp warmed his heart. He wrapped his arm around her shoulders. Gina was no stray, but Dorje had just let in his metaphorical cat.

---

AS DORJE'S arm slid around Gina, a sweet warmth spread through her. He was so big, so gentle, so lovable. She let herself lean into him as she took in the view. Evening sunlight washed the snow-covered glacier and its surrounding rocky peaks in a stunning orange glow.

"Dorje," she whispered, not able to raise her voice while taking in the beauty. It would have been like shouting in a church. "Your house overlooks Fireweed Valley? I can't believe you didn't tell me."

As he shrugged, his hand sliding on her shoulder sent a delightful tingle down her arm. "I couldn't share it with you when you didn't know about yeti."

Right. That. She wouldn't let it get to her. Dorje couldn't reveal himself to someone he'd only recently met, especially not a client.

She wasn't sure what kind of relationship might be possible between a human and a yeti. But the giant in goggles and a face mask had given her some serious pants feelings. They'd only grown stronger as they got to know each other. Was it wrong to have the hots for a yeti? No, definitely not. Dorje's grandmother hadn't thought so, and Gina surmised Nana had been a wise woman.

Gina adjusted her focus from the distance to the foreground. A wide deck wrapped around the house. "This side of your house must be full of windows to take advantage of the view."

He gestured to the hall off the open living room and kitchen. "The bedrooms upstairs and down all have sizable windows."

Her stomach fluttered at that news. The view would be even sweeter from Dorje's bedroom, his private space.

Several questions were on the tip of her tongue. *Do yeti need blankets on their beds? Would flannel sheets be too hot? And how about a tour of your bed and sheets while we're on the subject?* Her gaze snagged on a colorful pile across the room. Dorje's knitting—a much safer conversation topic. She gestured to the stack. "Will you show me what you've made?"

Dorje led her across the living room to a brilliant

rainbow of knitted goods. She sucked in a breath at the sight. "These colors are striking."

"Can't take credit. Most of it represents Nana's stash. She'd collected the yarn over the years for various planned and unfinished projects."

Gina held up a violet, triangular piece edged with a decorative border. The stitches were tight, uniform. "This is beautiful."

"A wrap," he explained.

"For the retirement center?"

He gave a nod. "Nana always had one over her shoulders, especially in her later years. I'm making a blanket out of the yarn you gave me. Some would prefer a lap blanket to a shoulder wrap."

"I use a blanket at my computer," Gina admitted. "My legs get cold when I sit for long periods."

Dorje sorted through his accumulated projects, explaining what he'd knit and where he planned to donate it.

Gina ran her hands over the lovely creations. He'd put a lot of time and thought into his projects. "How do you buy yarn? You can't head to a local shop."

"Not an option," he confirmed. "I order online—though currently I need more funds."

Mari's words came back to Gina. She'd said she

was glad to hear that he was working again. "My lessons are paying for your knit-a-thon production."

Dorje cleared his throat. "That's why I reached out to Eddie and took the job."

Didn't he have other guiding jobs as well? "My lessons are extra, right? You do other guiding with Mountain High?"

"I did." He pulled a knit hat over her head and draped a shawl around her shoulders. "I took early retirement starting last year."

She blinked. Retirement? That didn't make sense. He was young, strong, and a great instructor. Plus, why retire when he couldn't afford yarn? She let him double-drape her with another shawl. "I'm going to start sweating," she warned, running her fingers along the thick, cozy fleece. "But these are gorgeous, Dorje. It's very generous of you to donate your time and skill."

Big shoulders shrugged. "I have to do something."

"In your retirement?"

He looked a little flustered. "Knitting has been therapeutic. I find the repetitive motion calming and the items I produce will help others."

She took his hand, stopping it from draping her

in a scarf. "Mari mentioned you'd had a rough year. Do you want to talk about it?"

Dorje's aquamarine eyes didn't meet hers and his hand tensed in her grip. "No."

Okay then. Something weighed heavily on his shoulders. Was it grief from his grandmother's death or something more? Perhaps, in time, he'd open up. To change the subject, Gina motioned to her bag. "I brought my laptop. I could let you get back to your knitting and I'll start grading."

He led her back to the couch, where they both sat, falling into a comfortable silence. She put on headphones and opened her laptop to grade, while Dorje picked up his knitting and resumed his telenovela.

The giant, seven-foot yeti watched Spanish language soap operas while he knitted. She wouldn't tease him about it. It was too freaking adorable and clearly part of his self-healing process, one he didn't seem interested in discussing.

Gina finished well past sunset. They ate the left-over stew she'd brought, and the hour grew late. But she didn't want to leave. She packed her laptop and scooted towards Dorje as he watched his show. He set his knitting aside and wrapped an arm around her, pulling her against him. Heat from his body seeped into her. She let her eyes close, reveling in the comfort of being held by someone special. Some moments were simple perfection—like this one.

---

WHEN A LOUD SHOUT jarred Gina from peaceful slumber, it took her a moment to recall where she was. She hadn't taken a short snooze. She'd been deep asleep on the couch.

Large, furry arms tensed around her. She lay on her side, face to face with Dorje and flush against him. Her body hummed. *Oh, yes.* Being held in the arms of a sleeping yeti ranked number one on Gina's list of favorite things ever.

Dorje yelled again. Fully asleep, he called for his grandmother. It broke her heart. This poor man and his demons. But should she wake him?

When he jerked again, she stroked his arm. "Dorje," she said softly, "you're having a nightmare."

His whole body tensed in response, and a low growl rumbled from his chest. It might have been startling if he hadn't also pulled her in tighter against him in a delightfully possessive way.

Gina grinned. She wanted to be his.

After a moment, he muttered, "I don't dream."

"Nightmares aren't the same as—" Gina gasped as his big mitt of a hand slid from her hip to her backside and squeezed.

"Go back to sleep," he commanded.

Sleep? With his hand on her ass, her body stretched along his while heat and awareness coursed through her? Not possible. Gina freed a hand and found Dorje's cheek in the pale early morning light. Her fingers swept lower until they feathered across his lips. "I want to kiss you, Dorje."

He stilled but didn't open his eyes. Then he shifted, making it easier for her to reach her target—a sensual mouth the color of the sky in Van Gogh's Starry Night.

She slid her palm along his furry jawline and cupped his cheek. Then she leaned in and brushed a light kiss against plush lips. They were deliciously silky, a contrast to the short hairs of his beard that created an exciting friction against her skin.

Dorje's eyes briefly opened to half-mast, his hot gaze setting her on fire. He growled again. Every nerve ending came alive as the vibrations reverberated through her body. His mouth moved under hers in a delicious slide of their lips. His hand glided up her back until it tangled in her hair, triggering a flush of goosebumps down her arms.

She met his gentle nips and sucks, her body growing restless as the heat between them built. As if understanding her need, he shifted, rolling her body on top of his. His freed hand found her ass, snugging her up against the hard planes of his body as she lay on top of him.

Gina stifled a moan when their tongues met. His was textured and raspy but slick, new, and thrilling. She wanted more, a lot more . . . but a truck engine roared in the driveway.

Dorje stilled. "Fuck."

Gina glanced at the clock on the wall. *Oh shit!* She whipped her head back to Dorje. "It's nine a.m. I have to get home and teach." His eyes looked slightly out of focus and hazy with lust. She imagined hers looked similar. "We aren't done here," she said before giving him one last kiss. Not by a long shot. Gina had kissed her yeti and wanted more.

# CHAPTER TEN

There were only two people who owned noisy, oversized trucks and knew the code to Dorje's gate, Tseten and Mari. One of them was coming up the driveway.

Dorje reluctantly released Gina after one final kiss. As she tore herself away, his body stung with the loss of her heat and closeness.

While Gina raced to the bathroom, Dorje fumbled for his phone. His friends rarely showed up without texting. He clicked to open one unread message.

> Tseten: Breakfast casserole coming your way.

Since he'd been neglectful in responding to texts

and calls over the past year, his friends didn't wait for his replies before dropping by. He couldn't blame Tseten. He was nice enough to share a casserole that his cousin undoubtedly made. Pema was an excellent cook. It would be delicious.

As Dorje padded to the front door, his phone buzzed with a message.

> Tseten: Uh . . . Am I interrupting?

Tseten's truck idled in the driveway next to Gina's car. Instead of responding to the text, Dorje opened the front door and waved his friend inside.

Tseten, casserole dish tucked under his arm, walked in as Gina flew out of the bathroom.

She comically stopped in her tracks, socks sliding on the wood floor. Green eyes wide, her gaze bounced back and forth between the two yeti. "Gina, this is my friend, Tseten."

Tseten's face broke into a pleased smile. "I'm so glad to meet you." He thrust the casserole at Dorje, then enclosed Gina's small hand between both of his. "I've heard so much about you from Dorje and Mari."

"Y-you have?" she stammered, giving Dorje a

side-eye while greeting Tseten, the only other yeti she'd ever seen.

Dorje shrugged in return. "Our social circle is small," he explained.

Tseten waved a hand. "Don't worry, Gina, it's all been good. I'd love to hear about your tutoring business. I work remotely as well." He gestured to the covered dish Dorje held. "I brought breakfast. Do you eat meat? I think Pema added some caribou sausage."

Gina's eyes lit. "Wow, caribou. I've never tried it." She glanced to Dorje, then back to Tseten. "Sorry, I can't stay. I have to meet with a student."

Tseten's features drooped. He hadn't even known Gina was at Dorje's house and yet looked crestfallen to learn that she had to leave immediately. The extrovert's motto was always the more the merrier. "Dorje can put some in a bowl for you to take," Tseten suggested.

Dorje stiffened. Why hadn't he thought of that first? Was he jealous? Ridiculous. It didn't matter who had the idea as long as someone took care of Gina. "Yes, of course," he said.

As Dorje pulled out container and lid, Tseten said, "We may not know each other well yet, Gina, but clear your calendar for March fifteenth next year."

"Next year?" she clarified.

"My fortieth," Tseten explained. "Big party. Details to come."

Dorje couldn't help but smile. "Per Tseten, it's never too soon to plan a party."

Straight-faced, Tseten nodded. "It's not. It will take a lot of planning to get everyone up on the ice field."

Gina's eyes shone. No doubt he had her at "ice field."

"Consider my calendar blocked off. Thank you for the invitation, Tseten. And an early happy birthday to you for *this* year."

Gina shrugged into her coat. She grasped Dorje's hand as she took her to-go container from him. "Walk me to the door." It wasn't a request.

While Gina pulled Dorje into the arctic entry-way, Tseten grinned widely and made a show of busying himself with the casserole.

As soon as they were alone, she tugged Dorje's face to her own in a show of force that seemed out of balance with her size, and left him with a bruising kiss.

"Call me," she demanded, before rushing out to her car.

He didn't promise either way. He warred with himself about how close he should get to Gina. But, he hollered, "Drive safe," as she climbed into her cold vehicle.

Belatedly he realized he should have started it for her, warmed it up while she'd used the bathroom. When she disappeared down the driveway, he finally tore his gaze away.

Dorje pulled in an unsteady breath of frosty morning air, then returned to the kitchen. What the hell had he gotten himself into?

Tseten already had the casserole in the oven and the coffee going. "So," he began. "That looked like a sleepover."

Dorje collapsed into a chair at the table. "Unplanned. We fell asleep on the couch last night."

Tseten grinned and passed him a mug. "Looks like it ended well."

Dorje sipped at his coffee. "I shouldn't have let it happen." And yet he couldn't have stopped kissing Gina if he'd tried.

"Shouldn't have let what happen?" Tseten took a seat at the table while eyeing the old fruit and lacy mat.

"By letting her stay, I led her on. This can't go anywhere."

"You like her?" Tseten asked.

He did. That was the problem.

"If you're both into it, then what's the issue?"

"For starters, me." Dorje shrugged. "I haven't been in a good spot for a year."

"Gina might help you get out of that spot."

"What if I pull her into it?" he argued. Dorje did not want to dim Gina's brightness. She was a lighthouse to his storm. "Plus, she has some guy coming."

Tseten gave him a skeptical look, an eyebrow-raising. "That can't be serious when she's locking lips with you."

Dorje let out a warning growl, and Tseten raised his hands in surrender. "Mother Teresa herself would have known you'd been making out this morning and that Gina departed with an epic smooching session at your door."

A gusty sigh escaped Dorje as he leaned back in his chair. "Even if the other guy isn't serious, she should choose him. He can meet her family. Do human stuff. I'd hold her back."

Tseten crossed his legs. "There are ways around all that. Lots of yeti make it work."

"Says the guy whose girlfriend doesn't know he's a yeti."

Tseten looked away and shrugged. "Rosa doesn't live in Alaska. We've never shared pictures of ourselves. And what do you think would happen if I told her I was a yeti?" Tseten paused for effect. "I'd never hear from her again, and I could lose my work contract."

Dorje couldn't argue with Tseten on those points, especially considering Dorje hadn't planned to tell Gina about yeti. Tseten cared deeply for Rosa. Everyone hoped, for his sake, that it worked out somehow.

Dorje knew he needed to have a hard conversation with Gina and didn't want to talk about. He motioned to the oven. "I'll thank Pema for the casserole."

"She's stress cooking, going through her own human lover crisis."

Coffee went down the wrong way. "Pem?"

"Did you hear about that avalanche at the pass outside of Palmer? She and a family member of a Mountain High client got stranded when the avalanche buried the road. They sheltered in the A-frame. When I went to check on her, I walked in on them while they were next to naked and in each other's arms. So you being fully clothed with make-out hair is nothing compared to that. Jack's a great guy though. We're going skiing tomorrow if you want to come. You and Yeshe should both join."

Dorje looked up. "Yeshe?" Prior to the accident and Nana's passing, his brother contacted him via a satellite communicator. But with Dorje's failure to respond to messages this year, Yeshe reached out to Tseten instead. Dorje owed his brother an apology.

"Yeah, that's my other news. Your bro's coming to town for stove parts and a new sat phone battery. Dale's picking him up today. Better get his room ready. I insisted he stay with you this time."

A week ago, Dorje would have grumbled at the intrusion into his personal space. This was likely why Yeshe had messaged Tseten about his visit. But since lessons with Gina had started, his attitude had changed. Today, Dorje looked forward to seeing his brother.

He stretched his legs and laced his fingers behind his head. Yeshe would also give Dorje the perfect excuse to distance himself from Gina as they finished up her lessons. His heart might complain, but it didn't have a say in this.

GINA  PRACTICALLY  SPRINTED  to  the
retirement center on Monday afternoon. She needed
girl talk, and she needed it now.

Once she entered the cafeteria, she steepled her
hands in a plea. "Mari, I need help. And you need to
dish. Pack the tea caddy with something strong."

Mari wiped her hands on her apron. "Come on,"
she said, leading Gina through the double doors and
into the kitchen. "No alcohol back here, I'm afraid.
But I'll make you Tibetan butter tea." She plucked a
pot from the shelf and gave Gina a meaningful look.
"Now that you know about yeti."

Gina couldn't help but grin. She'd discovered a
secret world. She wanted to learn everything about
Dorje—and all yeti. But mostly Dorje. "Dorje said he
loves butter tea. Do all yeti drink tea?"

"Some do."

"Who taught you this recipe? Have you always
known about yeti?" Gina paused, looking at her
friend with a more critical eye, then asked in a low
voice, "Are *you* part yeti?"

Mari laughed. "So many questions. No yeti in
my family tree—that I'm aware of. And yes, I've
always known about them. My family is what they
call 'yeti-friendly.' We keep their secret, and help

them when needed. It's hard to navigate the human world when you're big and furry."

Gina watched as Mari pulled out salt, butter, milk, and black tea.

"I learned this recipe from my . . . friend. Nima is a yeti. But since he doesn't like the cold, his mother used to make him this tea, called Po Cha, to warm him on winter days."

"Is Nima," Gina repeated the name, trying it out, "from Wildwood? Have you known him and Dorje your whole life? What about Tseten? Do other yeti live here?" She held her face in her hands. "Sorry for the million questions. Yeti are real, and I've fallen for one."

Mari's eyes grew wide. "Oh my. You and Dorje must have had a good time Saturday night."

Gina's face heated at Mari's suggestive tone. "We kissed," she admitted, her knees going weak at the memory of their Sunday morning make-out session.

A grin stretched across Mari's face. "Girl, that's awesome!"

Gina groaned. "So nice. But I think it scared him. He texted to confirm our climbing lesson tomorrow and let me know that he's bringing his brother. But otherwise, he's been silent."

Mari swirled the pot of water. "I'm sure it's not you. Dorje hasn't been great about answering texts lately."

"He responded to all my texts before we kissed," Gina explained. "But he must have a lot on his mind. I mean, he understandably still feels his grandmother's loss."

Mari grimaced as she dropped the tea bags into the boiling water. "He was also involved in a mountaineering accident shortly after Nana died. It's better if he tells you the rest."

"An accident," Gina echoed, pushing up from the counter. "He didn't want to talk about whatever is bothering him, and I won't press him."

"He's come a long way this week since meeting you. It's a good sign that he's hanging out with his brother. Yeshe has a heart of gold. But he likes his me-time, which is why home is a remote cabin. He has a room at Dorje's, but this past year he's stayed with Tseten when he's in town."

Pieces were coming together—Dorje's focus on safety, his physical reaction after helping her down-climb the ice. Her gut ached at the thought that she'd caused him to relive a past trauma because of her recklessness. She pressed a hand to her forehead. "I can't believe he doesn't hate me for what I did to him last week."

"Hate you?" Mari grinned as she dropped butter and salt into the pot. "Just the opposite, I think. Thanks to you, he's acting like his old self again."

"I don't know what to think." Gina let out a deep sigh, forcing her shoulders to relax. "But I can't wait to see Dorje tomorrow, and I'm looking forward to meeting Yeshe." Knowing Dorje's family appealed to her.

Mari added hot milk to the pot, then poured the contents into mugs and handed one to Gina.

She gave her mug a swirl, staring into it with skepticism. "Did you mean to add sugar instead of salt?"

Mari sipped at her drink before smacking her lips and responding with a grin. "Nope. It's an acquired taste."

Gina sipped the hot brew, trying not to make a face. It was . . . different.

"How does Adventure Ted fit into all this?" Mari asked.

Gina nearly choked on her drink. "He's still calling me *Nina*. He arrives next week, right on time for spring break." She felt a little guilty for largely forgetting about Ted over the last few days.

"You don't sound excited, which is understandable if he still can't get your name right."

Gina shrugged. "I'm looking forward to having someone to go on an adventure with me over spring break." But now that she'd met Dorje, her excitement for Ted's visit had faded. Maybe if his texts didn't start with "Nina!" she'd feel better about it, about him.

Gina turned to Mari. "I guess I should be more optimistic. A lot has happened over the past week." In the short time she'd known Dorje, he'd changed her life, expanded it. She'd memorized the ten outdoor safety rules, understood ice climbing basics, had explored an ice cave. And she'd kissed a yeti and liked it. "Who knows what might happen this week?"

## CHAPTER ELEVEN

O n Tuesday morning, Dorje and Yeshe piled into Dorje's truck. Today he'd teach Gina a more advanced lesson at Granite Falls. Having Yeshe along provided the perfect distraction from his non-stop thoughts of Gina. It also meant no alone time with her. A good thing, or he'd likely start kissing her again.

Every time his mind returned to Sunday morning on the couch, Dorje's pulse thrummed, and his pants needed adjusting. He had to stop questioning what would have happened with Gina if Tseten hadn't shown up. Dorje was equal parts thankful and annoyed at his friend's timing.

But he couldn't continue flirting with—or kissing —Gina. A human and a yeti? Doomed from the start, at least in his family's experience. Plus, while she glowed like sunlight, he generated rain clouds. She was seemingly uncomplicated, while the murk in his mind was thicker than muck in a moose's bog.

Dorje cleared his throat as he backed into a spot. "Thanks for coming today," he said to Yeshe. "Gina is . . ." He trailed off as she pulled into the lot, her broad smile aimed directly at them. She parked and bounded out of her car, her crimson braids swinging with her enthusiastic movements.

Dorje turned to take in his brother's reaction. He expected the recluse to recoil at her exuberance. But a grin played at his mouth. "She's what?"

"She's . . ." Happy, energetic, hardworking, friendly. Too good for Dorje. "New to climbing," he said quickly as they exited the truck.

Gina jogged over and pulled Dorje toward her into a hug. She pressed her warm lips against his bare cheek above his beard in a quick kiss, and his skin heated. Their eyes met, her emerald gaze locking onto his. He was drawn to Gina and it both excited and terrified him.

"Hi," she said. Her voice dropped in a way that made it obvious her greeting was for him alone, and their relationship had eclipsed one of instructor and client.

While Dorje stood speechless, his senses clouded with confusing emotion, Gina shook Yeshe's hand. "I'm so glad to meet you. I have a twin sister, but we are so different. She'd never go ice climbing." She laughed. "But I'm so glad you're able to join us today."

Yeshe continued to grin. "Nice to meet you, Gina. I hear you're new to ice climbing. But, uh, now that I've met you, I understand why my brother's cookie jar is full again."

"Oh yes, Dorje's a wonderful baker," she gushed.

Dorje clenched his jaw. He'd made cookies. So what? Why was everyone making such a big deal out of it? He'd always baked for the retirement center. And now he kept the cookie jar full in Nana's honor. He might have filled it with the kind Gina liked, but she would *not* be coming to his house again, so that didn't matter.

"We'd better get to the falls," Dorje rumbled.

Gina leaped into action, racing back to her car to grab her gear.

Once she was out of earshot, Dorje growled at his brother. "Don't read anything into my cookie jar."

Yeshe raised his hands in surrender, an amused smile on his blue lips. "I don't need a full cookie jar to understand what's going on here. The way Gina greeted you said it all."

Dorje hoisted his backpack. "Nothing is going on."

"Whatever this 'nothing' is, it's good for you. You're out of the house and receiving kisses. The baking sheets are in use again, and you look a lot happier than the last time I saw you."

A scowl pulled at Dorje's mouth. "About today. Gina's last lesson is Thursday. I want to make sure she has certain skills to make good choices when out on the ice or in the mountains." He adjusted the load on his back. "Will you help me? These lessons have to count because I won't see Gina again after this week."

Yeshe pitched his voice lower as Gina approached. "Does she know that?"

Dorje shook his head, both to answer his brother's question and to silence him.

Gina nudged Dorje with her shoulder. His body tingled at the casual and deliberate contact. "You guys ready? I'm so stoked!" She didn't wait for an answer before charging down the trail ahead of them. He swore the air shimmered in her wake.

"She doesn't know," Yeshe observed as he fell into step behind Dorje.

Dorje grunted in reply. He lacked the strength to stop Gina's casual touches. They felt too good. His body and soul cried out for more. But for her sake, he needed to be more resilient and resist. He had to end this. They had no future together.

A NEW DAY, a new waterfall, and more time with Dorje. Gina should have been thrilled as she hit the high mark on her second climb of the day. But Dorje seemed distant this morning, less flirty. Was it because of his brother? Or was something else going on? She looked down at him and called, "You got me?" to indicate she was ready to descend.

Dorje took in the slack and Gina felt the tug on her harness. His aquamarine gaze met hers and he gave a nod. "Got you."

As Gina lowered down the ice, Yeshe said, "I'm going to follow the trail up the canyon to see if there's ice at Butterfly Falls."

Dorje paused, leaving Gina right at his eye level. The perfect height to kiss him. "I heard it was hard-hit during the last warmup," he said to his brother, "but it would be a great climb for Gina if the ice is good."

Gina spun herself around, the frozen waterfall sliding against the nylon of her jacket as she hovered several feet off the ground. As Yeshe headed down the trail she said to Dorje in a low voice, "Are you avoiding me?"

Before responding, Dorje glanced at Yeshe's retreating back. "We need to talk," he said as he turned to her.

"I agree." She leveled him with a hard gaze. "Why haven't you returned my texts?"

Dorje let out a sigh. "I've had a guest."

"Don't hide behind your brother. I-I thought . . ." she trailed off, suddenly unsure. "I thought we had fun together, that you'd enjoyed Sunday morning as much as I did."

Dorje tied off the belay, securing her in place. He shucked his gloves and cupped her cheeks with his bare hands. The soft, sweet caress sent mixed messages. "Gina," he said, his gem-like eyes searching hers. "I did. But . . ."

But. The word hit like a sucker punch to the gut. Gina didn't want to hear what he planned to say next. So she distracted him by pressing a slow, hot kiss to the palm of his hand, her lips lingering.

"Gods," he cursed under his breath. "You're

harder to resist than a patch of snow in July." He scowled but advanced on her.

"Why would you want to resist? We have a connection, Dorje," she said as he stepped closer. With the sweet satisfaction of victory, she wrapped her legs around him.

"Don't shred me," he warned, glancing at the sharp points of her crampons at his waist.

She huffed a laugh as she angled her feet away from him.

Their helmets tapped when Dorje leaned in, but he quickly maneuvered until his lips slid against hers. His firm hand at her nape held her in place while his mouth devoured and stole her breath.

She squeezed him closer with her knees, pressing herself against him. "This, Dorje," she gasped. "We can't ignore this." Kissing him made her feel whole, like her lifelong search had come to a final, brilliant end. No, not an end, a new beginning full of possibility.

He pinned her to the ice, and he held her there. She throbbed, captured between his hot body and the frozen waterfall. Their tongues met. Teeth nipped. She couldn't get enough of him. He dragged her jacket aside as his lips traced a scorching trail from her jawline down her neck. "Come over tonight," she breathed. "Have dinner."

Dorje hesitated, and a moment later, Yeshe's loud whistling and the sound of snow crunching under his boots echoed off the ice wall, signaling his approach.

She grabbed Dorje's hand as he pulled away. His passion-filled gaze shifted to a look of doubt. "Please, come over tonight," she asked again. She didn't want to beg but would if she had to.

He paused, then nodded. Gina couldn't help her smile and when she released Dorje's hand, he undid the belay knot and gently lowered her to the ground.

Her legs wobbled, and he caught her in his arm before quickly releasing her. "You made me weak in the knees," she whispered.

His eyes flared at her words, but he remained silent and busied himself with the rope as Yeshe came around the corner.

Gina tried to act normal. Yeshe had found more ice to climb. But she wasn't as excited as she should have been. Thanks to Dorje's kisses, she was more interested in conquering a seven-foot yeti than another wall of ice.

## CHAPTER TWELVE

Dorje stood at Gina's front door. Instead of driving, he'd walked. The distance and the darkness were no trouble for a yeti, and it allowed him to clear and calm his mind. But this meant that there was no approaching vehicle for Gina to hear. She wouldn't know her dinner guest lurked in uncertainty right outside her house.

He feared he lacked the strength to break things off cleanly with her. Her smile penetrated the walls he'd built around his heart and melted his insides. He was powerless against her advances. His body responded to hers with advances of his own. But he couldn't keep leading her on like this. It wasn't fair to her.

He should knock on the door and immediately tell her he couldn't see her again, that Eddie would teach her last lesson. But Gina had invited him to dinner. She'd invested time and effort into cooking, and he would share another meal with her—he wanted to. Plus, he'd brought a bottle of wine as thanks for the meal, and Yeshe had sent him off with fresh sourdough rolls.

Dorje also had a small gift for Gina. She'd inspired him with his yarn and needles—he'd been powerless to resist that too. And what he'd created was for her and no one else. He couldn't donate it.

Finally, he knocked.

The door opened, washing Dorje in a shaft of soft yellow light. Gina stood in the middle of that brightness, beaming at him. "I'm so glad you came."

She dazzled him, and he couldn't believe he was about to crush her.

Gina ushered him in, and he pulled the rolls from his backpack. He wasn't sure how to give her the gift, so he left it in his bag for now. "Yeshe traveled with his sourdough starter," Dorje explained. "He made fresh rolls for you."

Gina pulled back the cloth covering the rolls. Her eyes fluttered shut as she inhaled. "Heavenly," she breathed. "That was sweet of him."

But Dorje didn't want to think about his brother. "You have glitter on your eyelids."

She looked up at him through her lashes. "That's not the only place I'm sparkling tonight."

He caught a glimpse down her shirt's V-neck. When she moved, light glinted off sparkles on the soft curve of her mostly shadowed cleavage. Dorje swallowed hard. Gods help him. He'd need all his strength not to grab this woman—his woman—and take her against the wall. He'd been imagining it since he'd caged her against the ice that afternoon.

But she wasn't his woman. He couldn't confine her brilliance. She deserved more than him, more than a broken yeti and a complicated life half-lived on the periphery of human society.

Tearing his gaze from her, he turned to his bag and pulled out a bottle. "I brought a sparkling wine."

She squeaked her approval. "Are we celebrating tonight?"

"I didn't think you'd need an excuse for something . . . fun." Truth was, in his mind, a bottle of sparkling wine represented Gina in a sea of bland whites and over-hyped reds. Bubbly. Bright. Something special.

"You are one hundred percent correct." She passed him a kitchen towel to place over the cork when he opened the bottle, while she collected glasses from the cabinet. "I don't have flutes, so in keeping with this fun theme, we should drink out of these." She presented him with two small mason jars, swirls of fruit etched into the glass.

He filled each half-full and handed her one. She clinked her glass to his. "To a new adventure," she said.

Was she referring to Alaska, ice climbing, or him? He was afraid to ask. Dorje added, "And new skills."

She took a sip. But from over her glass, her gaze moved from his face to roam his body in a predatory way that made his muscles twitch. He wanted to teach her the skill of bedding a yeti. Gods, yes—no! No, that wouldn't happen. He couldn't let it. "Outdoor safety and ice climbing skills," he hastily clarified.

He gulped his wine. "Dinner smells delicious." The scent of home cooking permeated the small cabin. Dorje wanted to lose himself in the cozy and comforting atmosphere—and the urges they both seemed to be experiencing.

Pushing those thoughts from his mind, Dorje turned away. "Any word from your friend? Is he still on track to arrive this weekend?"

"Yes," she replied, but her voice had lost some of its emotion. "And I still have all next week off and plan to go winter camping and ice climbing." She glanced in his direction. "Covering up can't be very comfortable for you, but I'd love it if you joined us."

Dorje wouldn't be joining them. He'd hopefully armed Gina with enough awareness to make smart, informed outdoor decisions next week and throughout her life. He repeated what he'd said earlier. "We need to talk."

She set two plates on the table. "About the chemistry we have?" She immediately pursed her lips as if she knew that wasn't the direction he wanted to go.

Dorje sighed. "It doesn't matter. Even if I weren't a yeti, I'm not in a good place to start a relationship with anyone. My mind is a mess. And," he continued, holding out his furry forearms. "I *am* a yeti."

Her fingers teased his fur as they skated up his arm. "Chemistry *does* matter, and I don't care that we're not both yeti or both human. Let me support you, be with you while you work through your troubles, Dorje. You don't have to do it alone."

"I will not pull you into the pit that's been my mental state this past year. You don't deserve that."

"What if I choose it?"

His shoulders drooped. "I can't see you anymore after tonight."

"Can't or won't?"

"Both."

Bright green eyes flashed. "There's electricity crackling between us, Dorje. How can you ignore that?"

Iron will, he wanted to say. Though it bent and cracked the closer she came.

"I liked you when you were the faceless, masked instructor. My attraction to you has blossomed as I've gotten to know you, learned who you are, what you are." As she said this, her hands glided up his biceps, coming to rest on his shoulders. Her fingers lightly threaded through the fur on the back of his neck. "This is special, what we're feeling. Don't push it aside. Don't push *me* aside."

The pressure was there in her words and her hands. She gently pulled, willing him to bend down and kiss her. The powerful attraction between them was so thick, it was hard to draw in a steady breath.

He wasn't sure what snapped his will. The daring gleam in her eye? The intoxicating scent of her arousal? The idea of leaving without tasting her was unbearable. Why deny them both something more to always remember and cherish?

With a feral growl, Dorje scooped Gina into his arms. Her long skirt bunched around her waist as her bare legs came around him. He held one arm around her back, the other he slid under her smooth thigh. His fingertips skimmed the edge of her panties as he cupped her firm backside.

"Yes," she groaned before her mouth clashed against his.

He backed her against the ladder to her sleeping loft. They weren't quite stairs, but each step was wider than the rung of a normal ladder. He set her on a step, his torso forcing her legs open, her knees level with his upper body.

"Hang on," he commanded gruffly, as he ran the backs of his fingers along her inner thighs. They jumped and quivered under his touch, and she let out a whimper as she looped her arms around the railings.

It wasn't until he'd placed an open-mouthed kiss on the inside of her knee that he saw the shimmer. "You have glitter on your thighs." Her smooth, silken inner thighs gleamed at him, guiding him to her soaking wet core. Her arousal scented the air and darkened her pink, lacy panties.

Under hooded lids, her grin grew wicked, and

she spread her legs farther apart in invitation. "It's for you."

He needed all barriers gone. Now. Dorje kept his claws short, but they weren't useless. With a tug and a swipe, he shredded her panties.

Gina gasped and moaned, "Yes. Touch me, Dorje."

He intended to touch, lick, taste. Feast on Gina like it was his last meal. It would be their one and only time together. He wouldn't hold back.

---

GINA'S HEAD fell back when Dorje's slick, wide tongue licked the length of her pussy. As he focused his mouth on her clit, he eased a thick finger inside her. Despite what he'd done to her panties, she didn't feel a hint of claws, only sweet, unbearable pleasure. His other hand wrapped around her rib cage, thumb rubbing her sensitive nipple. It felt like he was everywhere at once and she loved it.

Tugging on the back of his head, she brought his mouth to hers. "Your face is covered with glitter," she mused, before sucking his lip into her mouth.

"You've marked me," he growled, his voice vibrating in a panty-dropping way.

But she'd long since lost her panties. Dorje, a fur-covered yeti with blue skin, had ripped them off with his claws as he had his way with her on a ladder. Holy frozen waterfalls. This was the hottest sex she'd ever had.

As their tongues tangled, his hand worked between her thighs, his oversized digit pumping in and out of her, while he circled her clit with this thumb. He kneaded and squeezed her breast before pinching her rock-hard nipple between two huge fingers.

When Gina let out an involuntary cry at the incredible sensation, Dorje's mouth descended on her other breast. Large blue lips sucked her through her shirt and bra before he lightly bit down on her super-sensitive nipple.

She whimpered again. "I'm close. So close."

Releasing her breast, he lowered his head between her thighs once again. He continued to thrust his finger in and out of her pussy, while his textured tongue circled and lapped at her clit.

She clenched around him, her mouth opening in a silent cry as she let go of the railing and gripped Dorje, riding his face as her climax built.

But right at the crest of her peak, he moved his

mouth. "Mine," he growled as large, sharp teeth grazed her inner thigh.

Stars exploded behind her closed lids as another tidal wave of pleasure—more intense than she'd thought possible—washed over her.

Her breath caught, then her body went limp, and she collapsed against the step.

Dorje withdrew his finger and carefully licked over the spot he'd bitten, his tongue soothing her sore flesh.

She threw her arms around his neck, clinging to him as she recovered. He held her against him in an iron grip, his chest vibrating in a thrillingly possessive growl.

*I want to be his.*

He continued to hold her as their hearts calmed, his hand gently running over the back of her head.

Eventually, he drew away, his eyes dark, like a deep emerald sea. Gentle fingers spread her legs, then traced over the red spot left by his teeth. His mouth opened, then closed.

"You *marked* me," she said.

His eyes grew wide as if he couldn't quite believe what he'd done.

Gina fisted a hand in his shirt. "Don't you dare regret this," she said. "I never will."

His confused gaze met hers. He was warring with himself. Why couldn't he see they should let this play out between them? Chemistry like this didn't come along every day. In the heat of the moment, he'd bitten her, claimed her, left his mark where others might see.

She hadn't lied. Gina had no regrets and would proudly wear that badge. She just needed to convince Dorje they should be together.

She rubbed small circles on the back of his neck. But as she opened her mouth to further reassure him, a playful "shave and a haircut" knock came at the door.

A loud voice called from outside. "Nina! I made it in record time. I'm early!"

*Fuuuck.*

## CHAPTER THIRTEEN

A predatory growl ripped out of Dorje's chest. Ted. Adventure Ted. "Did he just call you 'Nina'?"

Gina's eyes didn't meet Dorje's as her arms fell away from him. "Keep it down, he'll hear you. I've told him several times that it's 'Gina'."

Dorje saw red. Through gritted teeth, he added, "And he doesn't respect you enough to remember?"

She shook her head. "Don't judge. He can't get my name right, but unlike you he hasn't insisted that we're incompatible."

Dorje clenched his fists as he tried to control his anger, his frustration. If he weren't a yeti, he'd yank open the door and give Ted a lesson in manners. With his fists.

Dorje didn't want Gina grouping him with this piece of shit. An asshole who couldn't get her name right while insisting on a stupid, ego-inflating nickname for himself.

The knock came again. "Nina, you home?" Her phone vibrated on the table.

She yelled, "Coming." Then scooped up the tatters of her underwear before she rounded on Dorje. "Go up to my sleeping loft and keep quiet."

Dorje glanced at the bathroom, then back to her.

As if reading his mind, she asked, "What's the first thing you'd do after spending hours in the car?"

Right. The guy would probably need to use the facilities. Without a word, Dorje clambered up the ladder on which he'd just thoroughly sexed Gina.

On which he'd marked her. With his goddamn teeth. *Fuck!*

He sank onto her bed. Gina's scent surrounded him, filling his every pore. He buried his face in his hands. If hell existed, this would be his. Gina's sweet spring essence engulfing him without a hope of having her for himself.

Adventure Ted, despite being a dickwad, was human. He could provide Gina with the life she deserved.

The front door opened with a whoosh, and Gina

exclaimed, "Adventure Ted!" Her tone was a little too enthusiastic for Dorje's liking.

"Nina!"

Were they hugging? She was a hugger. The thought made him ill.

"It's Gina. With a 'G.'"

"Right, right. You keep telling me that, don't you?"

Her voice hardened. "Yeah. I do."

Dorje smirked. *Attagirl.*

"Gina. Gee-na. Gina," he said. "If I repeat it enough times, I'll get it." He paused, possibly when he saw the two place settings at the table and their wine. "Smells great in here. But it looks like you spilled something on your shirt. Did I interrupt your dinner?"

Her shirt was wet where Dorje had sucked her breast into his mouth. He licked his lips remembering the feel of her taut nipple through her shirt.

Plates clattered. "Oh, uh, must have splashed myself while doing dishes. I did cook but it didn't turn out very well. I'd rather eat out. Let's go grab a bite at Wildwood Brewery, and you can tell me all about your trip up the Alaska Highway."

"Brewery? I like the sounds of that. But, uh, can I use your little boy's room before we go?"

Dorje rolled his eyes at Ted's childish language. *He's not good enough for her*.

Gina directed Ted toward the bathroom, then her feet thumped up the wooden ladder and she appeared a moment later. The fabric over her left breast *was* dark, still wet from his mouth. Her eyes met his, flashing in what looked like her own anger and frustration before she pulled her shirt off.

With nimble fingers, she removed her lacy, pink bra. "I wore that for you," she whispered as she tossed the piece of lace onto the bed next to him.

Her bare breasts shifted with her movements. He swallowed hard, but otherwise sat transfixed, taking in the roundness of those breasts, the dusty rose of her nipples. Then her skirt came down. He knew she wasn't wearing panties, having ripped them off her. The sight of her fully nude curves took his breath away.

She paused, watching him watch her. It was as if she knew how her body affected him. What she didn't know—would never know—was how a yeti dick worked. His dick had just dropped from his sheath. Again. The thick length uncomfortable under his jeans.

For a split second, he imagined taking her hard

and fast—if she wanted it—while Ted remained clue-less down below.

But the bathroom door swung open, the doorstop reverberating as it bounced off the spring. "Say," Ted called out, "does this *brewery* source local products?"

That broke the spell. Dorje quickly adjusted himself as Gina grabbed a pair of panties from a dresser drawer. "When they can, but we're in Alaska. In winter," she said. With her back to Dorje, she pulled them on, her fine ass cheeks disappearing behind white cotton fabric that looked just as sexy on her as pink lace.

"What about fresh, local tuna?"

Next came a sports bra. She pulled that over her head, her perfect breasts sadly disappearing behind sturdy spandex. "Tuna is never local to Alaska, but they have salmon burgers with local kelp pickles."

She shimmied into a pair of jeans. When she paused to run a finger over the angry, red mark on her thigh, Dorje forced a dry swallow. What had possessed him to bite her? He felt both horrified and intensely proud of that mark. Unaware of his conflicted emotions, Gina quickly concealed the bite behind denim.

"What kind of oil do they cook their food in?" Ted asked.

"We'll have to ask," she called down before yanking a T-shirt over her head, followed by a bulky hoody.

Dorje approved. It hid her curves.

Fully clothed, she reached past him—slow and deliberate, it seemed—to snag a hair-tie off her night-stand. Her gaze locked on Dorje's as she pulled the flames of her hair into a tight bun at the back of her neck.

Gods, she was gorgeous.

Without a word to Dorje, she backed down the ladder. At the bottom, she said to Ted, "Ready? The brewery serves excellent food, and they make the beer locally—from imported grain."

Coats rustled, and they exchanged more small talk. The front door opened and shut. Then silence.

Dorje fell back on Gina's bed and buried his face in her pillow. How did he get into this situation? He shouldn't have come over. Certainly shouldn't have given in to his urges. He'd bitten her, for fuck's sake. Was that even a thing yeti did? He'd acted on instinct, caught up in the moment, drunk on her smell, her taste, her pleasure.

He pushed himself up. He had to get out of her cabin before he gave in to the urge to wrap himself in her blankets and never leave.

Dorje retrieved Gina's gift from his backpack, which was still resting against the wall by the kitchen table. He left the small parcel on her bed where Ted wouldn't see it. Gods, he hoped Gina didn't invite Ted to her sleeping loft, to her bed. Then he let himself out and trudged home in the dark, moonless night.

Gina had proven to be a temptation Dorje couldn't resist. So, he would remove himself from her —physically. He'd leave town. Give himself and Gina some space. He'd travel to Yeshe's cabin to help repair his stovepipe. It would undoubtedly be best for Gina.

---

WHEN GINA EMERGED from her shower, the sound of Ted's snoring filled the living room. Annoying. Just like his constant parade of stories about himself. Maybe he was tired and tomorrow he'd act more like the guy she met on the slopes. But she'd undoubtedly hear his snoring from her sleeping loft. A downside of having a guest in an open-concept cabin. At least she had a bathroom. In Alaska, some cabins were dry—no running water in the kitchen or a bathroom, with only an outhouse out back.

She climbed into the loft and perched on her bed. In the dim glow from her outdoor porch light, she adjusted her robe and inspected the love bite on her inner thigh.

This was a yeti bite, not a hickey. Dorje's canines were bigger and sharper than a human's, and he'd broken skin. It seemed like a marking. A scar she'd have for life. She traced the red tooth marks with her finger. The surrounding area had bruised, and it was sore.

She closed her robe. The ache didn't bother her. It couldn't compare to the pain in her heart. How could she feel so strongly about someone she'd just met? She couldn't imagine life without Dorje.

She collapsed on her bed, and Dorje's vanilla and cedar scent surrounded her. She squeezed her eyes shut, willing the tears not to spill. A pointless effort. They leaked out anyway.

As she rolled over, a small lump crunched beneath her. Despite her sleeping guest, Gina turned on her bedside lamp and picked up a small package. It looked like a rolled brown lunch bag tied closed with a yarn bow.

More tears trailed down her cheeks.

With shaky hands, Gina untied the bow, careful

not to unravel the orange and pink threads. Out from the bag slid a soft, beautifully knitted triangle scarf. Deep-violet strands mixed with textured blue and green yarn. Shot through all this were sporadic silver and orange metallic threads.

Gina choked back a sob. Dorje had sat in his house and knit this for her. She'd seen some of this yarn. They'd been leftovers on Sunday, but tonight they were a gorgeous scarf. For her.

She looked back in the bag and pulled out a folded note.

---

Gina,

I've wanted to try this lacy stitch for a while and you provided the perfect reason to do it. And now I can proudly say that I knit lace.

I've mixed a hand-dyed fireweed purple with novelty blues and greens—symbolic of the Fireweed Valley and the ice cave. I intended the silver and orange to be unexpected, just like you were in my life. A bright pop of color woven in. Something to make you smile, like you've made me smile.

I've stopped cursing goats for blowing my cover. Instead, I might stop hunting them. I'm grateful their ill-timed snow and rock shower brought us closer together. I will forever cherish the short time we had. It might seem like it's easy for me to turn away. It's not. It's the hardest thing I've ever done in my life.

This is the best thing I can do for you. I've changed the code to my gate, and I'll be going offline for a while. Eddie will teach your last lesson. I wish you the best, Gina.

With all my heart,

Dorje

---

Gina read and reread the letter until her vision blurred with tears. Why was he so determined to leave her? When her eyes finally dried, she studied the fine stitches in the lace and the deliberate placement of color. Besides all his other skills, Dorje was an artist.

Gina slid under her covers, curling into a tight ball in the middle of her bed. She'd gone from a mind-blowing orgasm with a guy she was crazy about to a snoring guest in her living room. Her heart ached to be with Dorje. She tucked the scarf, the most precious gift she'd ever received, under her cheek, feeling more alone than ever before.

## CHAPTER FOURTEEN

The next morning dawned gray. It fit Dorje's mood—bleak. He and Yeshe sat in the cab of his idling truck parked on a private airstrip. They waited for Dale, a yeti-friendly pilot, to arrive and fly them to Yeshe's cabin on Little Caribou Creek.

Yeshe sipped coffee from a travel mug. "While I appreciate your offer, I can repair the stove without help. You don't have to travel to my cabin."

"Are you that eager to be by yourself again?" Dorje joked. "The forecast is for twenty below zero on the creek. Repairs will be a bitch in that weather. They'll go faster if you have help." Yeti were biologically built for the cold, but the actual work would be challenging in winter weather. Materials failed at that temperature—adhesives and plastics became brittle, and batteries quickly died. And even yeti found it more comfortable to wear gloves when handling metal as the mercury bottomed out.

Yeshe's mouth quirked. "Are you sure you aren't just looking for an excuse to run away from Gina?"

"I'm not running," Dorje said. He wasn't. He just needed to put some space between himself and Gina. That wasn't running. It was removing himself from the red-headed temptation. "Eddie's covering her last lesson. That leaves me free to help you. Plus, I hardly know Gina. I only met her last week. There's nothing to *run* from." He fought a cringe. Sure, they hardly knew each other and yet he'd bitten Gina after making her come, and his chest ached whenever he thought of her.

"I don't have any experience with a relationship like this, but it seems like duration doesn't matter when you've met the right person."

"Gina and I don't have a relationship. Plus, I could never be the right person," Dorje argued. "She's bubbly, full of life, ready for adventure. I'm not in a good headspace, and we're yeti and limited in the adventures we can experience."

"But those limited adventures might appeal to her," Yeshe argued.

Dorje let out a sigh. "I don't want to limit her.

We should go our separate ways now. That way she'll have more opportunities for travel, exploration . . . everything in life.

Yeshe didn't look convinced. But as far as Dorje knew, Yeshe'd had little interaction with women. Yeshe asked, "But what about you?"

Dorje raised an eyebrow. "Me? This from the hermit yeti who lives in a remote cabin by himself?" Yeshe lived alone because he didn't think he was worth anything to anyone, thanks to absent parents who'd scarred the guy for life. Dorje shrugged. "I survived this year. I can make it through the next."

The approaching plane caught their attention.

Yeshe drained his coffee. "I appreciate your offer of help, but it's not too late to change your mind."

But Dorje had made his decision. He looked forward to the change of scenery and the slow pace of life on the frozen creek with Yeshe. And by getting out of town, he would be hundreds of miles from Gina and her spring break adventures.

---

GINA LACKED the usual spring in her step when she entered the Wildwood Retirement Center on Monday. Despite having the week off, she'd kept her tea date. She desperately needed girl talk, more insight into the minds of yeti, and an escape from Ted.

Mari had already arranged the tea on a table when Gina came in. Except it wasn't tea. It was hot chocolate with mini marshmallows and a bowl of freshly whipped cream. "I thought you could use something special today," Mari explained. She reached into her apron pocket and produced a small flask. "I even smuggled in some peppermint schnapps."

Gina leaned in to give her friend a quick hug. "You. Are. The. Best," she declared, then promptly plunked into a chair. She poured a healthy glug of schnapps into her mug, then added both mini marshmallows and whipped cream, even if they were redundant. This wasn't the time to sacrifice small pleasures. She closed her eyes and took a slurp, licking at her white, creamy mustache afterward. "I needed this," Gina sighed as she finally shrugged out of her jacket.

Next to her, Mari sucked in a breath. "Your scarf is gorgeous. Did you get it at Bore Tide Boutique, that new place next to Wildwood Bakery?"

Gina's traitorous eyes welled with liquid. She shook her head. Words were hard.

Mari's eyes went wide, and she leaned in examining the gift. "Did Dorje make it for you? It's so intricate, and the colors are stunning."

Gina nodded as she found her voice. "There's meaning behind each color. I fell for an artistic, lace-knitting yeti who gave this to me as a parting gift." She let out a watery laugh and wiped away a stray tear.

Mari offered Gina a comforting hug. "A parting gift? That sucks. I'm so sorry. I knew he left town, but I wasn't sure where things stood with you two."

Gina's eyes went wide. "He left town?" She should have known. "Did he go to Yeshe's cabin?"

Mari nodded. "And he updated his gate code. I don't have it."

"He told me he'd changed it, which stings. He doesn't trust me to not show up."

Mari arched a brow. "Would you have gone to his house?"

Gina huffed a harsh laugh. "Yes," she admitted. "And maybe it stings so much because he already knows me so well. I would have tried to convince him we don't need to cut off our relationship entirely." She set her mug down with a thud. "He's being dumb."

Mari fingered the slim chain around her neck.

"In my experience, some folks are really dumb when it comes to their hearts and feelings."

"Agreed," Gina sighed, relaxing some as the liqueur and companionship eased her tense muscles. "Thanks, Mari, for all your support. I feel like we never talk about what's going on in your life. Next Monday, it's all about you."

Mari took a big gulp from her mug. "I have little to talk about, presently. And we'd need more than a flask of schnapps if we unpack my baggage."

Gina paused and stopped herself from demanding to know more now. But she sensed it wasn't the right time. "I'm here for it when you're ready," she pledged as her phone blared the beginning of Beethoven's Symphony No. 5.

Mari snorted. "Did you change Ted's ringtone to that?"

Gina bit her lip. "*Adventure* Ted. He'll never hear it, right? If he calls or texts, it's because he's not with me."

Mari grinned. "I like the way you think. It's not going so well?"

"He falls into the 'dumb human' category. He got bent out of shape when the bakery didn't have fresh mango scones. But he's very focused on buying local and rejected the locally sourced lingonberry muffins."

"Does he realize mangos don't grow in Alaska—or anywhere close by?"

Gina sighed. "He's a jumble of contradictions. But we still have a trip planned. I wanted to give you the details. We're going up to Fireweed Glacier and traversing to Little Bear Valley. We'll camp there and climb ice in that area. We plan to come back Friday night. Consider us overdue if we don't return by Saturday."

"Noted. Send it to me in an email?"

"Already done." Her phone buzzed again. "T—Adventure Ted is ready for a pickup." She gave Mari an apologetic smile. "I gotta run."

"Stay safe," Mari called as Gina zipped her jacket and left.

Mari had warned her not to let her FOMO get her in trouble by breaking her heart or fracturing a leg up on a mountain. Thanks to Dorje, safety was at the forefront of Gina's mind. Her legs would be sound, but she couldn't say the same for her heart.

## CHAPTER FIFTEEN

B luebird skies and brilliant sun greeted Gina on the morning she and Adventure Ted started their trip. But Ted exited Gina's cabin like a vampire about to go up in flames. "It's so bright. I don't have sunglasses."

Gina paused as she arranged the gear in the back of her car. "What about in your truck? You drove thousands of miles to get here."

He rolled his eyes as if she were being outrageous. "Through Canada and Alaska in the middle of winter. I didn't need sunglasses."

Northern days were shorter in winter, but it wasn't like they were above the Arctic Circle. Plus, it was almost spring equinox when the whole damn planet received twelve hours of daylight. She gave her pack a shove into the corner of her trunk. "You need them now. We'll swing through town on the way to the trailhead."

Gina could hear Dorje's bittersweet voice in her head reciting the top ten essentials list. Sun ranked tenth, but it was equally important as the others. The March sun wasn't as bright or high-angled as in mid-summer, but Ted would need sunglasses for the snow glare alone. Why hadn't he thought of it himself?

Gina pulled the small, laminated essentials list from her pocket. She suddenly became sentimental. She didn't want to part with something Dorje had given her. But he had moved on and Gina needed to as well. Besides, Ted could use some guidance, just as Gina had when Dorje had found her solo climbing with little awareness of the risks.

"Have you heard of the ten essentials," she asked, passing the card to Ted.

His gaze flicked to the card, but he didn't take it. "Those? Of course. Every outdoors group has its version. When you've seen and done as much as I have, you move beyond lists."

Gina blinked as warning bells sounded in her head. Was it too late to cancel this trip? Dorje would tell her if she didn't feel right about it, she shouldn't go. Safety first, listen to her gut.

But as Ted said, he *had* seen and done a lot. Maybe she was being overly cautious. One thing was for certain, though. Ted annoyed her. But did she have anyone else willing to travel to Little Bear Valley for a few days of ice climbing? No. So she'd go with Ted.

While she didn't identify it as such, Gina ran through the ten essentials list with Ted on the way to the trailhead. They both seemed well prepared, aside from his lack of sunglasses, and they purchased a pair in town as planned. Also, Ted had an emergency locator beacon if worst came to worst.

They left Gina's car at the Fireweed Valley Trail-head and made their way toward the glacier. Per Dorje's warning, Gina had confirmed with the Chugach Avalanche Center that the avalanche danger was low before crossing through Fireweed Narrows. When they came to the spot where Gina had learned that Dorje was a yeti, a sense of intense longing triggered a dull ache behind her sternum. Dorje consumed her thoughts again—as he seemed to do ninety percent of her waking hours and one hundred percent of her dreamtime.

Had he and Yeshe already fixed the stove? Did

temperatures plummet as low as forecasted? Was Dorje thinking about her as much as she was thinking about him? Or had he already moved on? That possibility depressed her.

Access onto the glacier proved easy, which Gina had read it would be. They walked up without needing ropes. They spent little time on the glacier and instead walked on the snow-covered side moraine to reach Little Bear Valley in the afternoon.

As they entered the valley, Gina disagreed with Ted on a location to pitch their tent. "If we place it where you're suggesting," she cautioned, "our tent will be right at the bottom of this narrow gully. If snow unloads and shoots down the channel, our tent will get hit and buried."

"But this is most scenic," he argued.

She gave him a crisp smile. "We can't enjoy the scenery if we're buried in an avalanche."

He rolled his eyes but agreed to continue to a safer location for camping. The views were equally stunning, and the avalanche risk was nearly zero.

Ice draped the sides of the valley walls. In her trip planning, Gina had learned that water seeped from the rock inconspicuously during summer. In winter, it formed frozen rivulets that increased in size until they melted again in spring. This time of year, the ice was fat and great for climbing.

After pitching the tent, they explored the area without their heavy packs. With their base camp set up, some of the stress of the trip melted away, and Gina allowed Ted and his fantastic tales to pull her into his thrall once again. He'd traveled the world. His experiences appealed to Gina, and her thirst for adventure and learning new things.

On a scale of one to ten, few would deny Adventure Ted a fat ten—at least on looks and charm alone. But when Gina woke the next morning with his sleeping bag curled around hers, she eased away from his body. She'd rather choose the cold side of the tent than sleep next to anyone other than Dorje.

Distance might work for him, but it wasn't working for her. She couldn't get him out of her mind. And when she compared Ted to Dorje, Ted held a distant last place.

Day two with Ted mostly went as planned. They chose easy climbing routes that allowed for a top rope. Despite his worldly experience, it was becoming apparent Ted had over-advertised his skills. Gina couldn't fault him. She hadn't been honest with him either—she was only beginning to grasp the sport.

On day three, the weather turned. Light snow started midday. By early evening, fat flakes obscured the view across the valley. "We should return to the tent," Gina suggested. "We're more than a mile from base camp, and the snow isn't letting up. Our tracks are filling in, and the tent might be hard to spot if it's already covered in snow."

"That's a sound plan. Let's do that right after I climb Runaway Bride." Ted gestured to a frozen stream of ice to their right that cascaded over jagged rock like a trailing tulle veil.

Gina tried to blink away the snowflakes sticking to her eyelashes. "You think my plan is good, but you still want one last climb?"

He didn't respond as he angled toward the ice to see if they could set up a top rope. In his haste, he dropped his pack and didn't attach crampons to his boots before scampering up the rock outcrop next to the frozen waterfall.

Suddenly, Ted's left foot slid out from underneath him. The fresh snow may have covered patches of ice where he stood. His right foot was on solid rock. But it couldn't take his sudden weight shift or the torque of his off-kilter body.

Gina watched, horrified, as he went down, grabbing in vain at the rock wall. The sheer slab beside him offered nothing. His arms flailed, one of them slamming into the ledge.

Ted screamed as he tumbled down the icy rock face.

---

THE SHARP CRACK of creek ice in the frigid temperatures broke the endless quiet of Yeshe's cabin retreat. That, and the hammering and swearing of two yeti attempting to install a rooftop stovepipe during winter.

Yeshe's one-room dwelling was the quintessential Alaska log cabin. Piles of snow shoveled from his roof and front walk made for easy access to the problem stovepipe. As predicted, the repair process challenged their skills and patience thanks to the sub-zero temperatures. But Dorje couldn't complain. He'd volunteered for the job, and for brief moments, it took his mind off Gina.

He sat straddling the peaked roof, one leg slung over each side. Dorje focused on the far horizon, not the work in front of him. The glow of the sun dipped beneath a layer of clouds, producing a golden-orange blaze.

Gina carried that same brilliance. She'd soon be

in Little Bear Valley if her plans worked out. He pictured her strong and sure, chipping her way up ice, marveling at the surrounding beauty. Everything seemed to please her.

Except their last moments together.

With effort, Dorje tried to push Gina and those painful memories from his mind. Again. Failing, he turned to Yeshe and asked, "Have you ever heard of Brunswick Stew?"

Yeshe held his hand out for the cordless screwdriver. Dorje pulled it from inside his warm jacket— it wouldn't operate at these temperatures otherwise —and handed it to his brother.

"No, can't say that I have." Yeshe positioned the drill and drove a screw into the flashing around the stovepipe.

"It would use up several of the frozen cans of food—tomatoes, corn, lima beans."

When Yeshe traveled to Wildwood his canned goods had frozen solid. They'd stored them in Yeshe's cache until they could consume or discard the swollen cans.

"Did Gina make it for you?"

Though phrased as a question, it wasn't. Dorje was that transparent. "She said that her family made it with rabbit. Do you have any hare in the cache?"

The drill whirled as Yeshe pushed in another screw, then he slid the drill into his own jacket. "Top left-hand side. I can manage the rest of this if you're making supper. I'll call down when you can use the stove."

The hare made a fine stew, but it didn't compare to Gina's version. They ate several meals from the large pot. Yeshe made fresh batches of skillet sourdough biscuits each evening to go with it.

The cabin was once again cozy after fixing the stovepipe. As the days passed, Dorje busied himself with checking all the ice fishing holes on the creek. Then he drilled new ones. He hauled and chopped firewood until his hands ached, and he stopped for fear he wouldn't be able to knit.

No matter what Dorje did to keep his mind off Gina, it would bounce back to her, like a compass settling on north. And after a week in the wilderness, unease fell over him as darkness descended on the cabin one evening. He picked up his knitting, a comfortable distraction. But he kept dropping stitches and eventually set his needles aside.

Wood curled under Yeshe's knife. "Something wrong?" he asked, not looking up from his willow burl.

Dorje rubbed the back of his neck. His fur stood on end. "No, I . . . I don't know. Just a bad feeling."

Yeshe motioned to the small, portable radio on the shelf next to Dorje's chair. "It's almost time for Arctic River Relay. Maybe someone has a message for us. Or check the sat communicator."

The communicator showed no new texts, so Dorje turned on the radio. In remote Alaska, where cell towers didn't exist, River Relay both entertained and acted as a lifeline in emergencies. Dorje tuned in to the radio channel and returned to his knitting.

The broadcast that evening included reports of overflow on winter trails mostly used by snowmachines. But there were no messages for him or Yeshe. This should have eased Dorje's mind. It did the opposite.

Later that night, as he lay on the built-in bench that doubled as a sleeping platform when Yeshe had guests, he willed his eyes to shut. When he finally drifted off, his dreams were of Gina. He held her firm, curvy body against him in a possessive and protective embrace, fingers tangled in her blazing red hair.

## CHAPTER SIXTEEN

T ed lay in a crumpled, moaning heap at the base of the waterfall. Moaning was good. Dead and unconscious people didn't moan.

Gina and her sister Emma had taken first aid and CPR as a teenagers when they'd started babysitting. A lifetime ago. Why hadn't she enrolled in that wilderness first responder class in college or when she moved to Wildwood?

Was this the type of situation Dorje had experienced? Did he try to prevent it from happening again by emphasizing a safety-first culture? He'd armed her with knowledge, and she'd tried to make smart decisions. But she'd still come out here with Ted.

Gina assessed the situation. She stood on packed snow, but Ted lay on the ice at the base of the falls. It wouldn't be safe to dash over to him, only to slip and fall herself. "Hang in there, Ted," Gina yelled as she quickly removed her crampons from her pack. She pulled off her gloves—it would be faster to attach them with bare hands—and promptly slashed her palm with the sharp spikes.

*Fuck!* Pain radiated from the center of her hand as blood dripped into the snow. She grabbed a fistful of the white stuff in her injured hand and squeezed tightly, essentially putting ice and pressure on the wound.

She let out a slow breath as the snow in her hand melted. Having a calm, level head was imperative in this situation. The ABCs of first aid flipped through her head. Ted's moaning hadn't stopped—a good sign, all things considered. And it meant "A" his airway wasn't blocked, "B" he was breathing, and "C" he had a pulse.

Gina finished putting her crampons on and shoved her now numb and injured hand into her glove. She strode through the new snow. Her footing sure with the crampons, even on bare patches of ice that were wet from seeping water. The flakes fell so fast now that Ted already had a dusting on his red jacket as she slid to her knees by his side. "Where does it hurt?"

"Everywhere," he moaned, the word drawn out, presumably to emphasize his extreme discomfort. It had the opposite effect on Gina. It relaxed her a measure. Being dramatic meant he likely wasn't knocking on death's door.

While cradling his arm, he said, "I think I broke it."

She believed it. She'd seen his arm hit the ledge, but then he'd also plunged down the side of the rock and landed hard on the ice. At least he wore his helmet, the strap still latched under his chin. "Can you move your fingers?"

He cried out. "Yes," he hissed through clenched teeth, then in a whiny tone added, "Why did you make me do that?" He sounded like a cranky child.

Because that's what they asked people to do in movies. She didn't admit it out loud. He'd probably be less flippant if he had a compound fracture—not that a broken arm wasn't extremely serious. Snow fell in large clumps. The daylight would soon fade, and they were miles from the trailhead and medical help.

"Can you sit up?"

With her help, he moved to a seated position. If he could get to his feet, he could walk back to the tent or maybe on to the trailhead, though she'd first have to get crampons on his boots.

She checked in with him to see if his lower half hurt. When her gloved hand brushed his ankle, he shrieked and collapsed—slowly, so as not to hurt his arm.

Gina sat back as the gravity of their situation sunk in. Ted couldn't get back to the tent under his own power, let alone the trailhead.

They needed a rescue.

"Activate my locator beacon," he begged. "It's in my pack."

"Right, uh huh." Gina exhaled slowly to keep the panic at bay as she crossed the ice to Ted's pack. The large compartment held a coiled climbing rope and nothing more. He carried no extra clothes for layering. No extra food. No emergency supplies—not even a stray bandage. She pictured Dorje shaking his head in disgust.

She turned his ridiculously empty pack inside out. No locator beacon. Either he'd stored it in the tent or forgotten to pack it. She'd thought little about owning a personal locator device or satellite communicator. Until now.

As Gina's gaze flit back to her climbing partner, she formulated a plan and put it in action. She wrapped Ted in her emergency blanket like a burrito and tugged him through the snow to their tent. The route included a steady decline and gravity worked with her as she pulled.

Dragging Ted made the trip take twice as long, but eventually, Gina found the tent in the dark. She beat off the snow, then opened the door fully to heave Ted inside.

As soon as they were in, Gina emptied the stuff sack that held the rest of Ted's belongings. "What does your beacon look like?" She turned to her climbing partner to find him chugging the last of their water. To her extreme annoyance, more seemed to drip down his chin than hit his mouth.

"It's bright green," he said, then narrowed his eyes. "No, orange."

Gina sifted through his extra clothes, which only included a wicking T-shirt and long underwear. He'd also packed a portion of their remaining food, toiletries, an extra hat, and liner gloves. No beacon or emergency gear. He didn't even have matches or a knife. How had he traveled the world and live to talk about it?

"It's not here," she said, then paused. Another major item was missing. "Ted, where's the fuel can you were supposed to pack? We've been using the one I carried."

"It weighed too much. It didn't fit our minimalist effort."

Gina stilled, resisting the urge to scream. *Our minimalist effort?* They had discussed nothing of the sort. Through gritted teeth, she said, "What the *fuck* are you even talking about?"

"We all need to consume less."

That might be true, but in this context, it made no sense. "Ted, if we don't have enough fuel to melt snow for water, or hydrate our dinner, your minimalist effort might very well contribute to our untimely deaths."

Ted calmly responded, "I'm at peace with that."

With effort, Gina resisted the urge to strangle her companion. Instead, she exited the tent, forcefully yanking on the zippers to shut him in. She filled their cooking pot with fresh snow, melting it until they ran out of fuel. That left one warmish water bottle for Ted—he was injured. And one cold, slushy bottle for her—she'd shortly be hiking down the trail, which would elevate her core body temperature. She could handle icy water. She had to. Didn't have a choice.

Gina left Ted wrapped in both their sleeping

bags, with the warm water bottle and food within reach. She also left him in complete darkness—he hadn't brought a headlamp, and she needed hers to coordinate a rescue.

Unencumbered from Ted, Gina hit the trail. She carried a light backpack and her phone tucked into a chest pocket to keep it warm and prevent the batteries from dying. She ran several miles, fueled by adrenaline, anger, and frustration. At the end of the Fireweed Glacier moraine, her phone displayed one bar of service. Gina dialed 9-1-1.

***

IN HIS DREAM, Dorje held Gina tightly in his arms. But the sound of a plane roused him, and he realized he clutched an old blanket to his chest instead of the woman he longed for.

Dorje's eyes popped open. "Dale's early."

Yeshe sat up, his gaze focused out the window. They watched as Dale's plane buzzed the cabin on approach to the creek, where he'd land on the ice and snow using skis.

While Yeshe lit a lamp, Dorje sprang to action, adding more wood to the stove. He couldn't shake the feeling of unease that had started last night.

Gina's well-being was at the forefront of his mind. Was Dale's unscheduled visit related? Would his thoughts always go to the worst place because last winter had been so tragic?

As if he sensed Dorje's unease, his brother said, "Dale's probably taking advantage of a weather window." Then he ducked outside to meet the pilot.

Dorje repositioned the kettle to heat water before pulling out the instant coffee and mugs. He warmed a tray of leftover biscuits on the hot stove and placed a jar of wild raspberry jam on the table.

Dale and Yeshe entered as Dorje was setting out a stack of plates. The dishes clattered onto the table when he spotted the serious looks on their faces. "What's wrong? Has something happened to Gina?"

Something had to be wrong with Gina or one of their close friends to warrant such concerned looks.

Dale pulled off his hat and stepped closer to the warming stove. "I don't have many details. I only know that there is an active rescue in Little Bear Valley."

"Where Gina planned to camp."

Dale gave a nod. "Could be other people in the valley. It's spring break. Denzin, Eddie, and Tseten were part of a rescue team that hiked in last night. Mari called, sending me to get you—just in case."

Dorje was familiar with the process—too familiar. His mind flashed with images from last winter. Getting the call in the field. Reworking plans. Charging toward the accident site. Howling wind and blinding snow. Already full of grief from his Nana's passing, his failure to save the injured mountain climber had sent him spiraling.

He closed his eyes to stop the dark pull of his thoughts while he absently rubbed at his chest, a dull ache there turning acute. "Thank you for coming. I'll gather my things."

He turned, his thoughts racing. A million questions peppered his mind, but Dale wouldn't have answers. There were so many things Dorje wished he'd said to Gina or done differently where she was concerned.

It was one thing to know that she was alive and well in the world—even if she wasn't with him. It was another thing . . . No. He wouldn't think it. Couldn't think it. She was the sun itself. How could the earth continue to rotate if she wasn't there to dazzle?

Dale accepted a biscuit and jam to go, then they were airborne within minutes. Dorje skipped both caffeine and food. He might regret it later but had no stomach for it currently.

The flight back to Wildwood seemed twice as

long as normal. It felt like they were a bird caught in a strong headwind, aloft and hanging mid-air. There were no views, no sun, only endless monochrome terrain that hardly seemed to move beneath them. A land covered with snow and ice. Gloom as far as the eye could see.

Dorje could do nothing but think—for better or worse.

When he'd walked away from Gina, had he made the right decision? He'd abandoned her. Left her with no alternative but to forge into the wilderness with this Adventure Ted. And Dorje had no confidence in Ted.

If something happened to Gina, it would be Dorje's fault. He shivered despite his puffy jacket and the fur on his body. He'd tried to protect her, but that might have led to her physical harm.

He'd been wrong. So wrong. And so stupid. He'd let someone as precious as Gina slip through his fingers.

He would beg her for forgiveness. Plead for a second chance. She'd made him feel happy. Hopeful. Alive. And she hadn't hidden her feelings for him, despite that some might consider him a monster based on looks alone.

As Dale approached the private airstrip in Wildwood, Dorje scanned Fireweed Valley. Dense clouds hugged the mountain peaks. Dorje's cold vehicle sat on the edge of the airstrip below them. Mari had parked next to him, and a plume of exhaust curled out of her truck.

What did it mean that she met the plane—was it a good sign or bad? His gut triple-knotted with anxiety and dread.

Mari climbed out to meet the taxiing plane. "They found them," she yelled as soon as Dorje had opened the plane's door. "They've taken Gina to the Wildwood Health Clinic."

"Is she . . .?" Dorje couldn't finish the sentence.

Mari shook her head. "Don't know. I don't have a status for either of them."

Dorje didn't bother unloading the small bag he'd traveled with. Details weren't important right now. Getting to Gina was his only focus. "I have to go to her."

"I know." Mari motioned to her truck. "Get in. Goggles and a neck gaiter are on the passenger seat."

Dorje flung himself into Mari's truck. "Drive fast," he pleaded. "And thank you." Perhaps Mari understood what Dorje had been blind to. Gina was a once-in-a-lifetime treasure. This time, he wouldn't let her go.

## CHAPTER SEVENTEEN

Gina woke at a strange angle, propped up, half sitting. A soft yellow light cast a glow on the walls of her small . . . hospital room? Someone squeezed her hand and brushed her hair back from her face.

"Gina?" The deep voice rumbled low, and she felt the vibrations tingle through her body.

"Dorje?"

"I'm right here." His warm, calloused hand lightly squeezed hers as his fur teased her bare forearm.

She closed her eyes and focused on the sensation of his touch and the solid, warm bed. Relief washed over her in welcome waves. *I'm safe.* Not in the wet, cold, and dark of Little Bear Valley.

The valley. Her eyes popped open, and she sat up. An IV attached to her other hand tugged on her skin when she moved. "Where's Ted? Is he okay?"

Dorje's hand tightened around hers. "They transferred him to a hospital in Anchorage. He's stable. You saved him."

She sat back on an exhale as memories of their ordeal flooded through her head. The fall. Snow. Dark. Waiting. Then leading the rescue group to their tent.

She glanced at the IV. "Am I okay?" Then she gave her head a little shake. "Also, where am I?"

"The Wildwood Health Clinic. You're exhausted and dehydrated." He turned the hand he'd been cradling palm up. "And you needed stitches."

Once she set eyes on the bandage, she noticed a subtle, painful throb in her hand. "Caught it on my crampon when I was helping Ted."

"And you didn't tell anyone," Dorje chided. "Medics didn't discover this until they pulled your bloody glove off after you helped carry Ted out."

"I—I didn't carry him out, but I pulled him for over a mile to the tent."

"You what?"

"It's a long story," she began, pausing when a noise outside the room caught her attention. She quickly turned to take in Dorje. A gaiter coiled loosely around his neck, and a pair of goggles rested atop his head like sunglasses. "*You're* in the health clinic." Her chest seized in panic. Anyone could walk in and discover him.

"By your side. Where I . . ." His deep voice cracked. "Where I should have been."

Gina sat fully upright. "Someone will see you."

He shrugged, his aquamarine gaze holding hers. "A calculated risk. The clinic is small and has some yeti-friendly staff. It's more important that I'm with you."

Gina's heart thudded at his words—even if she wasn't yet sure what to make of his presence.

Someone rapped on the door. "It's Margie," the person announced with abrupt efficiency.

With a gasp, Gina moved in her limited capacity to help Dorje cover, but he calmly answered the knock with, "Come in. Gina's awake."

While Gina mouthed, "You know her?" the door opened just wide enough for a dark-haired nurse in purple scrubs to slip in.

She checked the monitors before turning to Gina and asking, "How are you feeling?"

Gina had participated in an all-night rescue in the middle of a snowstorm. Then she'd woken up in a clinic to find the yeti who'd broken her heart at her bedside. And he gripped her hand like he never wanted to let go. "A bit overwhelmed," she answered honestly, only then realizing the nurse was probably not asking about her mental state. "I'm okay."

"She woke a few minutes ago," Dorje added.

"You two know each other?" Gina couldn't help but ask.

"Margie's our local midwife," Dorje answered. "Her grandmother was present at my birth."

"I'm a registered nurse," Margie clarified as she typed a note in Gina's file. "Yeti refer to me as the midwife because my grandmother was a midwife. She cared for yeti, though in general, yeti need little medical care. I've taken over her practice."

Margie caught Gina's gaze and continued, "Aside from your hand, which will be sore, we didn't find any other injuries from the last twenty-four hours. You have a series of lacerations on your inner thigh, but those are healing."

Dorje's marking. While Gina didn't have regrets, Margie had to know exactly how Gina received the, uh, lacerations. She didn't dare glance at Dorje. Her flaming face had to be crimson enough already. She jerked a nod at Margie.

The nurse continued without batting an eye.

"We'll send you home with antibiotics to prevent infection in your hand." She typed something on her laptop before reaching to squeeze the IV bag. "You're almost finished with these fluids."

As quickly as she'd entered, Margie slipped from the room.

A silent beat passed. Dorje ran a finger across Gina's forearm. "Are you okay with me being here?"

She nodded and clutched his hand tighter. His presence confused her, but she didn't want him to go. She felt more complete, at peace, with Dorje at her side.

"I owe you an apology," he continued. "I'm sorry, Gina. So sorry." His voice was nothing more than a gravelly whisper, and it sounded like it pained him to speak. She glanced over at him and troubled eyes, the color of tempestuous seas held her gaze.

"I've had a hard year," he explained. "Never felt so alone. I've been in a dark place. I've blamed it on my failure in the mountains, the guy I couldn't save. He had a family who loved him. Their devastation had a profound impact on me. I realize now that the incident served as a trigger. I'd been grieving already. Nana had only been gone a few months when the mountaineering accident occurred."

He paused before offering a wobbly smile. "I'm a

seven-foot, male yeti. The death of a stranger or an elderly woman shouldn't impact me so deeply. But it did. Nana was the one person who had been there for me my entire life. My rock, my stability. Even when our roles reversed, and I cared for her, and she eventually transferred to the retirement center, Nana was a force." His voice cracked. "I loved her."

Apparently, broken hearts could fracture further because Gina's splintered for Dorje. She wanted to hold him. Comfort him.

He continued. "I reached out to Mountain High only because I'd run out of yarn. I didn't think I was ready to be part of society again, leave my dark place —or even if I could." He huffed a laugh. "Our first meeting tested that. You on the ice wall without experience or protection."

"*I* tested you." She hadn't meant to, of course.

"*The situation* tested me. I made it through. You were strong, sure, and irritatingly positive and likable. I looked forward to our next meeting."

He heaved a sigh, thumb tracing slow circles along the back of her hand. "Gina, you've been like the sun to me. Your brilliance penetrated that dark, as if you'd reached in and yanked me into the daylight. It left me dizzy but feeling more like myself —maybe better than my old self. I wanted to both hold on to that feeling and run from it. It was the best and most terrifying.

"I was scared. I still am. You seemed too good to be true. I was afraid losing you would break me, feel even worse than the loss I experienced last year. So I ended it before that happened. I thought it would be best to prevent potential future damage *and* let you live a normal human life."

Dorje's raw confession brought tears to Gina's eyes, blurring her vision.

"I also wanted to protect you from the darkness that had consumed me whole. To me, you're the brightest star. I wouldn't want to dim even a fraction of your light. Plus, what kind of life could you live with a yeti? Imagine all the half-truths you'd have to tell. The things we couldn't do together. That's not fair to you."

"Dorje . . ." Didn't he understand that if they were together, their light would never fade?

"But it's too late."

Gina's chest tightened. What was he saying? She clutched his arm. "No, Dorje. It's not—"

"I mean too late to cut my losses. I fell for you. I thought I could change my feelings by putting distance between us, but they've only intensified.

When I thought I might have lost you, I—I saw that void again and realized what an idiot I've been."

He ran a hand over his face, then growled. "I marked your fucking body. I hadn't planned that. It felt primal. I wanted to make you mine." His steady gaze bore into her. "I want you, body and soul. And if you still want me after how I treated you, then me, and my heart, are yours for the taking."

Gina's own heart thumped so fiercely she feared the machine monitoring her pulse might emit a warning alarm.

Margie's entrance interrupted their private moment, exposing Dorje's vulnerability. The nurse appeared oblivious to it.

"You can go home now," Margie said, as she made a note on her laptop before closing it. "But you shouldn't be alone for the next twenty-four hours. Is there someone who can monitor you?" The nurse's gaze focused on Gina. She didn't assume that Dorje would be her caretaker. The decision was Gina's.

But her heart had made that decision when she'd woken to find Dorje at her bedside. He might have some groveling to do, and she'd let him, but she wanted to give this loveable guy another chance. She had to. He held her heart, and she couldn't live without it or him.

"Dorje will take me home with him," Gina announced, not caring that he hadn't offered. After his apology, she trusted he'd be willing. "He'll take care of me while I recuperate."

To Gina's surprise, Margie smiled. "He's an excellent nurse," she said. "You should have seen him with his grandmother."

While more tears sprung to Gina's eyes, Dorje let out a gruff cough, as if he still wasn't completely comfortable with his tender, emotional side.

Margie dug into her pocket and passed Dorje a set of keys. "Dale brought your truck to the clinic. Use the backstairs to go out and warm it up. I'll bring Gina down in ten minutes."

Dorje leaned in, his lips brushing Gina's cheek in a soft kiss. "Thank you," he said. "You won't regret it."

Gina had no doubts.

---

DORJE HADN'T REALIZED that an invisible weight had been smothering him until he'd confessed all to Gina. The weight had lifted and her positive response gave him hope. He'd also never been so sure of what he wanted—a future with Gina. If she'd have him.

Margie walked Gina out through the clinic's front door. Dorje jumped down from his truck to meet them, his gloves, gaiter, goggles, and hood in place.

"Nurse Dorje," Margie ordered, "your patient needs a hot bath, clean clothes, and plenty of sleep."

Gina flashed him a smile as he helped her into the truck. "And a massage, Nurse Dorje."

"You going to call me that all weekend?" he asked in a gruff voice, but a warm sensation spread through his chest, and he fought a grin. He looked forward to caring for Gina—and he'd willingly massage her from head to toe.

She lifted a shoulder. "We'll see how far it gets me."

It didn't matter what she called him. He'd answer yes to all her requests, and she likely knew it.

Gina yawned as they pulled out of the parking lot. "Let's go straight to your house. I can pick up clothes tomorrow. Margie told me that Ted will probably be in the hospital for a couple of days."

Dorje didn't argue. The day had slipped away, and his patient needed sleep. Once at his house, he turned up the heat before getting Gina oriented in the bathroom. While she filled up the tub and soaked, he put on a kettle of hot water and reheated soup from the freezer. Then he tackled his bedroom, stripping the bed and changing the sheets.

By the time he had the covers turned back for her, the tub glugged as it drained. Gina emerged a short while later, padding past Dorje's bedroom and into the kitchen, where he watched the stove. She'd twisted her hair into a towel and wore an oversized Mountain High Guiding Service T-shirt. The shirt hit above her knees and hid her sweet, curvy body.

But Dorje couldn't stop his gaze from traveling up her bare legs. He shoved aside memories of them wrapped around him at her cabin the previous week. This was not the time.

Based on the smirk she presented him with, Gina had a pretty good idea where his mind had gone. She unraveled the towel, then used it to squeeze water from her brilliant red locks before hanging it over the back of a kitchen chair. "I have a confession, Dorje."

He stilled. She probably had a lot to say to him. He'd take it.

"I just used your toothbrush. Given my last twenty-four hours, the gross factor of using yours was lower than my desire for a minty-fresh mouth."

His lips quirked, and a chuckle threatened to

escape. "I appreciate your honesty." He'd tell her later that he had spare toothbrushes. "Would you like some tea and soup? I have a pot heating on the stove. Smells like Mulligatawny, which means it came from Pema. I didn't label it before putting it in the freezer." Over the past year, he hadn't bothered with such things.

Gina sniffed at the air. "It smells wonderful, but I'll stick with tea. Tomorrow, I might eat you out of house and home."

Dorje made two cups of mint tea and sat at the kitchen table with Gina.

She cradled her mug in her good hand and reached for him with the other. "I have some other things to say to you, Dorje, and I want to say them now." A yawn interrupted her. "Before I fall asleep."

His heart thudded, and he squirmed in his chair, uncertain what would come next.

"I appreciate your honesty. I understand that this past year hasn't been easy for you, and you've experienced tremendous loss in your life. Thank you for sharing this with me. I'm pleased that you feel you can confide in me—because you can. If life becomes hard again, know that what you share with me will never be a burden. I'd like to be there for you. We can work through tough times together."

He nodded, a cursed lump forming in his throat.

"I need to be honest too, though—and not only about your toothbrush. You really hurt me, Dorje. More than anyone ever has. I think that's because I feel more for you than I have for anyone else. Ever."

He swallowed hard at her words. Gods, he hated the pain he'd caused her, but a glimmer of hope formed in his chest.

"You've compared me to the sun. If I am, then it's true that I'm not shining as bright. You took a piece of me when you left my cabin last week." She paused and sipped her tea. "I'm upbeat by nature—I recharge like a solar panel. And I think in time, with you, I can be whole again."

Tears glistened in her eyes, undoubtedly matching his as she said, "You offered me your heart, Dorje. I accept. I'll protect it. Cherish it. Thank you for trusting me with it."

A low rumble sounded in his chest. He felt like he'd burst from the overwhelming emotion that rushed through him. "Gina," he whispered. He wanted to scoop her into his arms, crush her to his chest.

"Whether or not you know it, you already have my heart. People have teased me for suffering from FOMO—and perhaps I do. But I think when I met you, I found what I'd unknowingly been searching for, what I'd been missing."

Dorje couldn't hold back. He pulled Gina into his lap and pressed a kiss to her forehead before he cradled her to his body. "I didn't know what I had. I promise to heal what I broke and to never, ever, take your heart for granted again."

Gina's lips brushed the bare skin of his cheek above his beard. "Thank you, Dorje." She snuggled into him, then smothered another yawn.

What kind of nurse would he be if he didn't insist that his patient rest when she needed it? "I made up my bed for you. Can I tuck you in before I shower?"

Gina slipped off his lap and stood, but kept her hand linked with his. "Will you join me in bed afterward?"

Sleep with her? His heart pounded. Is that what she meant? "I can sleep on the couch. You can call out to me if you need anything."

"No. I want you in bed with me."

He let out a growl. "I sleep in the nude."

A mischievous smile lit up her eyes like two dark emeralds. "Good. I'll be waiting."

She was asleep, of course, by the time Dorje slid under the sheets to join her. The previous night's storm had cleared, and a sliver of moonlight shone across the bed. He propped himself on his elbow and took her in. Gina laid out in his bed, her hair like a scarlet aurora dancing across his pillow. Gods, he was the luckiest person in the world. This woman had trusted him with her heart. He would never, ever abuse that privilege again.

Gina wiggled toward him as he settled under the covers. He spooned her body against his and held her tight, determined to never let her go.

## CHAPTER EIGHTEEN

Gina awoke sprawled across Dorje, her chest on his, arm wrapped around his broad expanse, and leg draped over his middle. Her shirt rode high. With nothing on underneath, she lay exposed and bare against him. A shiver of pleasure passed through her as she shifted and Dorje's fur tickled against her sensitive parts. They were awake, alert, and interested.

She could easily ignore the ache from her injured palm when she had other things to focus on—like her big, yeti cushion. And god, did he feel good against her skin.

Also, he'd promised to care for her heart. With her *emotional* needs met, she was ready to satisfy some *physical* needs.

She moved again, and Dorje's arms tightened around her, one across her back, the other resting on her bare thigh. He lightly ran his hand along her leg in a sweet caress of his leathery fingers. His touch was both tender and arousing, and Gina couldn't help but slide her hips against him once more.

The chest she lay on vibrated with a growl. "I'd like to wake up like this every morning with my sunshine grinding against me." He moved his hand from her back to push a strand of hair from her face. "How's my patient feeling this morning?" His aquamarine eyes searched hers as he ran his fingers through her hair once more in a loving gesture.

"Excellent," she said. "I feel like exploring."

His body shook with a silent laugh. "Of course you do. What do you want to explore?"

She lightly traced her hand across Dorje's solid, fur-covered chest, loving the warm tickle against her uninjured palm. "You."

His grip tightened, and he growled, his body rumbling under her. From this angle, his large canines slipped over his bottom lip. He looked fierce. Was fierce—and yet she knew his soft, caring side.

She wanted both. She wanted him.

"I want to know you. Touch you. See all of you." Gina rose to her knees beside him and drew back the blankets. She ran both hands across his torso as she took him in. The fur on his chest was the same color as that on his arms and legs. Pure white, occasionally mixed with light gray. In places, it took on a blue undertone from his deep cerulean skin beneath.

Before meeting Dorje, she could never have imagined such a magnificent body. Well-defined planes of hard muscle lay under his fur. She traced the contours of his pecs, then bumped fingertips over rippled abs. He grunted in response, his hand moving to grip her leg.

"Take off that shirt," he demanded. "I want to see you too."

With a coy smile, Gina arched her back, thrusting out her chest as she dragged Dorje's old T-shirt up her body, across tight, aching nipples, and over her head. The quick intake of his breath grati-fied as she exposed her breasts.

She returned to her explorations, his muscles twitching under her fingertips as she dipped below his navel. "What's going on down here, Dorje?"

"Yeti aren't exposed," he said in a deep voice while his caressing hand lazily inched up her leg. "We aren't like vulnerable humans, with their soft parts flopping about." He paused as her fingers snuck lower. "I know you've been dying to ask—"

"What does a yeti dick look like?" Her lips quirked, and she huffed out a laugh. "It's an essential part of the Q and A. But that's not the question I want answered." She turned her head to meet his gaze. "I only want to know *your* dick. What does *it* look like, taste like, feel like in my hands, my mouth, my pussy?"

"Gods, Gina." His eyelids lowered to half-mast, and his grip tightened on her body. "Move your hands lower, to my sheath."

She did as he instructed, finding a bulge where the root of a human's dick would be. With slight pressure, she massaged the area.

He groaned. "If you keep that up, I'll drop."

Gina paused, a thrill shooting through her. "Drop?"

Dorje gave a silent nod, his eyes shut, hand tense on her thigh. "Swell and expand from my sheath."

She grinned and doubled her effort, rubbing and stroking between his legs. A moment later, she was rewarded when the fat, glistening tip emerged. She bent forward and circled her tongue around the midnight blue head of the largest cock she'd ever seen.

Opening her mouth wide, she took him in, only to hear Dorje exclaim, "Gina, I—" His words became an incoherent grunt of pleasure as he suddenly filled her mouth, bumping the back of her throat as his long, thick shaft fully emerged.

With watering eyes, she ran lips and tongue along his length, savoring the unique, salty taste of him. Then she wrapped her hands around his girth. The sight of his massive, deep-blue cock made her throb with need, adding to her wetness. But . . . "You're huge."

In his baritone voice, Dorje responded, "I'm a yeti." As if that explained it all. And maybe it did. "Hung like a yeti" would be a popular term if more people knew about them and their anatomy.

Instead of moving between his muscled thighs, Gina threw a leg over Dorje. She stretched herself wide to straddle his torso and presented him with her backside. He hoarsely whispered her name as she bent forward and licked him from his sheath to his dark, bulbous tip. She sucked him into her mouth again as she also teased him with eager hands.

Exposed as she was, Dorje's hands slid up her legs, fingers rubbing, fur gliding along her quivering skin. He palmed her ass cheeks and squeezed. "You're drenched," he declared as two of his large fingers slid through her wet folds and grazed her throbbing clit.

She paused as she bobbed up and down on his length, her body trembling in response to his touch.

"You like that." Less of a question from Dorje and more a declaration of intimate knowledge gained. He continued to stimulate her small nerve bundle.

Gina moaned her response, squeezing him tighter with her hands and lifting her hips higher, giving Dorje better access. He took it, teasing her nub while he slid a finger inside her.

Gina's eyes fluttered shut, and she hummed her pleasure around the fat cock in her mouth as he slid another finger through her wetness. A moment later, he eased that second oversized yeti finger into her pussy. Her body pricked with heat as he stretched and filled her. Sweat beaded across her shoulders. He went slow, spearing her until his knuckles hit her ass.

She pushed back against him, loving the pressure, the fullness, and knowing what it prepared her for. She kissed the fat tip again, sucking away a bead of precum as he pumped his fingers in and out of her.

Already strung tight, heat raced through her body. She hadn't intended to come this way. But when he rubbed her clit with his other hand, a powerful orgasm hit her without warning. Gina let out a cry of pleasure as her body spasmed with release.

She collapsed forward onto Dorje's thigh, her body a quivering mess.

He slid his fingers from her body, then rubbed tender circles along her legs and down her back. He said nothing, but a distinctive sound came from his throat. Not quite a growl, more like a purr. It soothed, this sound of contentment. It made Gina want to curl up against him and never let go.

But she wasn't done. Once she caught her breath, Gina turned around and leaned into him. Their gazes locked as her breasts brushed against the fur on his chest. The prickle and tickle against her sensitive skin was a sensation she'd never tire of. Gina slowly brought her lips to his.

When they made contact, Dorje's arms came around her. He rasped her name between crushing kisses.

Making out with her yeti was something Gina planned to spend hours doing in the future. But right now, she wanted more. She pulled back. "I'm ready for act two."

"Gina, you'll be sore," he grimaced. "And I don't have any condoms."

"I'm on the pill." She held up a hand, not

wanting him to think it had been for Ted. "I have been for years to keep my cycles regular. They're in my jacket—haven't missed one." She gave him a sly grin. "And you weren't worried about soreness when you marked me. Plus, I plan to do this a lot, so let's start now."

"Fuck," he whispered on an exhale. Eyes glinting like gems, he scooped an arm around her and rolled so she was under his massive body. He reached between her legs, tracing the mark, and rumbled, "Mine." Then he dragged the tip of his massive cock along her folds.

Gina's eyes nearly rolled back, but she pressed a hand to his chest. "In act two, I ride my yeti."

Dorje leaned down and pressed a wet kiss to her left nipple. "In what part of your plan can I finally lavish your bare breasts with caresses?"

Gina giggled and arched her back. "I didn't write it into act two, but you may revise the script."

His lips came around her nipple, and he sucked it into his mouth. "So thoughtful," he said, kissing his way to her other breast. "So flexible in your plans." While he showered her chest with attention, his hands moved lower, dipping between her legs. "Still so wet," he murmured.

"And ready." She arched against his hand, aching to feel him buried inside her.

Gina attempted to roll Dorje over. Moving a brick wall would have been easier. He chuckled at her efforts before turning and lying back, his hands interlocked with hers.

It wasn't easy to straddle a yeti—her legs spread wide again—but Gina looked forward to experimenting with positions. She slid along his shaft, coating him with her wetness before positioning him at her entrance. His dick was larger than his fingers, but she was so ready, his tip glided right in. Their eyes locked as she slowly sank onto his length until he filled her completely. The slight sting of the stretch quickly turned to ripples of pleasure.

Dorje squeezed her hand. "Are you okay? Is this okay?"

A flush crept up her body, and she could see the red blooming across her bare skin. "So good. Now I'm not only marked by you, I *am* yours."

---

THE AIR LEFT Dorje's lungs at Gina's renewed declaration. She'd already told him he'd captured her heart, but this felt different. Symbolic. Like mating.

A fierce sense of possessiveness swept over him. What this woman had been willing to go through mentally and physically—for him. Even now, she'd impaled her small body on his giant cock. He wanted to thrust up into her but fought the urge, making sure she had complete control of the situation.

The feel of her around him was like nothing he'd experienced before. And the sight of Gina's flushed body stretched wide to take him made his dick twitch with need.

"I feel you pulsing inside me," she moaned, her hand reaching down to rub her clit. The blush crept across her cheeks, and her eyelids drooped. Then she began to move.

Dorje had worried that she would still feel poorly in the morning and need to be in bed all day. They might be in bed all day, but they wouldn't be resting.

Of course, Gina would immediately rebound. Immediately be ready to learn—explore. And after all he'd put her through, she wanted to explore . . . him. Dorje wasn't sure what he'd done in a past life, or his current one, to deserve her. But he would never, ever push away her brightness, her smiles, or her enthusiasm again.

Dorje let Gina set a rhythm. He moved with her,

slowly grinding up into her. It took all his control not to flip her over and thrust into her deeply—they could try that another time.

"Ohhh," she moaned. "I never come twice, but this is going to happen." Her gorgeous breasts bounced as she rode him, her fingers between her legs furiously rubbing her pleasure spot.

Later, he'd learn everything that pleased Gina. "Let go," he begged, his own orgasm building. She was so much—so tight, enthusiastic, and all his. His pleasure began to coil.

As if sensing this and in tune with his body, Gina cried out, "Please, more."

At the first pulse of her pussy clenching around him, Dorje thrust into her. His hips rising to meet hers again and again, his body shaking with the most intense climax he'd ever experienced as he released deep inside her.

"Dorje," she cried, her face exquisite with release as she broke apart at the same moment.

As soon as his lungs filled with air again, he sat up—still fully inside Gina—and wrapped his arms around her. Their chests pressed together, heaving as they caught their breath. He ran a hand down her hair and then kissed her temple. "Amazing," he murmured as he held her close, never wanting to let her go.

Gina giggled. "I'll say. You made my eyes roll back in my head. If my vision is blurry later, I'm blaming you." She teased, but placed an achingly tender kiss on his lips. "I'd also have no regrets."

Dorje brushed his lips against hers in return. "If anything, sex with a yeti will improve your eyesight," he joked before easing back to the mattress, bringing Gina with him. "After a short nap your vision might be better than twenty-twenty."

She nestled into his chest. "Seriously, Dorje. That was unlike anything I've ever experienced." She slid her hand to his shoulder and whispered, "I'm so happy to be with you."

Dorje's chest clenched. He felt the same. Given his recent loss of a loved one, his feelings for Gina exposed his vulnerabilities. But also made him feel lucky, so damn lucky. He shouldn't fear a yeti-human relationship. That's what he'd had—with Nana—until last year, and he couldn't imagine his life without it. A relationship with Gina would be different, of course, a partnership.

His breath caught as he realized what he wanted more than anything. "Move in with me," he blurted. "I want you here. With me. Always."

Green eyes made a slow blink, then a dazzling smile spread across Gina's lovely face. "Yes," she said. "I want that too."

Dorje blinked back something that suspiciously felt like tears. "I love you, Gina."

She propped herself on her elbow, her smile still radiant and shining down on him as her small thumb gently brushed at the corner of his eye. "Thank goodness, because I love you too, Dorje." She cradled his cheek with her palm. "I think we're going to be very happy together."

With Gina in his life, Dorje couldn't imagine his future any other way. "So happy," he agreed with all his heart.

# EPILOGUE

"I'll tell you the same thing I told Mom and Dad. Dorje is a very private, small-town guy. He doesn't like to have his picture taken, and he's not on social media."

Emma, Gina's sister, grew silent on the other end of the line before saying, "You can't deny your poor track record with men. I'm only looking out for you since your latest wanderings have taken you to Nowhere, Alaska."

Gina made the mistake of sharing her new address with her family and telling them she'd moved in with her boyfriend. Perhaps she should have gotten a post office box and kept quiet about Dorje.

"You can be impulsive. Like when you dropped out of college—"

Gina rolled her eyes and cut her sister off. "For the record, taking time off from college in my early twenties to travel and work has only made me a better person."

"You cleaned bathrooms at a resort."

"And now I leave tips when I stay in hotels. Besides, not everyone wants the corner office with a view." Emma sucked in a breath and Gina felt guilty for her dig.

"Emma, I'm fine—better than fine. I'm really happy."

The line went silent again. Emma claimed to be happy with Derek, her boyfriend, but Gina had her doubts.

Emma sniffed. "Okay, don't tell me then. Derek and I will meet Dorje this summer when we come up to canoe the Arctic River."

"Huh, what?" Gina glanced at her phone as if the signal had gone bad, and she hadn't heard her sister correctly.

Emma was urban. When she vacationed, it was all-inclusive. Also . . . *Fuck!* Gina glanced at Dorje, who'd just taken the last cookie sheet out of the oven.

He'd warned her it would be hard to explain their relationship to her family. She didn't think she'd have to worry about it for a while. None of her family had any interest in Alaska. She thought they'd worry about her less if they knew she'd moved in with her boyfriend.

Emma continued. "It's something we're trying. The Y provides lessons."

"Canoeing lessons?"

"We paddle around the pool. Practice tipping. What? You think you're the only one in the family who can be adventurous?"

Gina had to stop herself from responding, "Yes". And couldn't help but ask, "Is this a guided trip?" Anyone could change, and she wanted to be supportive of her sister. But unless there was someone on a gravel bar opening a bottle of wine for Emma and Derek at the end of the canoeing day, Gina had a hard time believing they'd sign up for it.

"Of course, but that doesn't mean we won't have to paddle our own boat. It's adventure travel. Right up your alley."

At a cost too-high for Gina. Adventure travel to her was a bumpy bus ride with locals and buying food out of someone's dented cooler.

Across the room, Dorje tapped his wrist, silently reminding Gina that they needed to leave soon.

"Good for you, Em. That sounds like a great trip. I gotta run."

"Send a picture, something about this guy," her sister demanded.

Gina put Emma on speaker as she rambled about searching court records—she'd find nothing on Dorje, of course. But Gina pointed to her phone and mouthed to Dorje, "Say hi."

He pointed at his chest as if to say, "Me?"

She nodded vigorously.

"Dorje's right here," Gina interrupted. "Say hi to my sister Emma."

Dorje let out a breath and repeated, "Hi, Gina's sister Emma."

"What? Was that him? His voice is deep. Rumbly."

"And you are on speaker," Gina announced. "We're late for an appointment. Love ya, bye." Gina ended the call before her sister could respond.

She let out a sigh, then caught a whiff of the baked goods. "The cookies smell delicious."

"Last batch is for you. Grab one while they're hot."

Gina padded into the kitchen and stopped short. Her chipless, chocolate chip cookies included multicolor dots. Her gaze flicked to Dorje and she flashed him a wide grin. "Confetti sprinkles? I love it!"

He shrugged, a smug smile playing on his lips. "I knew you would."

She broke apart a soft, warm cookie and took a bite. It practically dissolved in her mouth. She slid an arm around Dorje and hugged him. "Delicious. Thank you." She looked around. "Do you need help, or is everything packed up for the retirement center?"

Dorje pointed to two boxes filled with knitted items for the fundraiser. Next to that lay a wrapped cookie tray. "We're all set. Mari said she'd only be around until five."

While Gina recounted the call with her sister, they put on light jackets for spring weather before carrying the boxes to Dorje's truck. "My parents are happy I moved in with someone. My sister is suspicious of you and wants more information—I don't know why she'd care. And . . ." She paused and heaved a sigh. "My sister and her boyfriend are coming up to float the Arctic River next summer. Her boyfriend, Derek, is a jerk," she added. "Em's too good for him."

Dorje loaded the boxes into the truck and pulled her to him. "We've got a few months to decide how best to tell her about yeti." He rubbed a hand across Gina's back and his lips curled into a smile. "As I recall, you were going on an adventure with some jerk in Alaska too. But that worked out pretty good for the two of us." He tipped her chin up with his fingers. "We'll figure it out."

Gina huffed a laugh as she slid her arms around Dorje and laid her head against his chest. Her anxiety instantly faded with his calm attitude. With Dorje by her side, it *would* all work out. "We will," she said. "Together."

---

I hope you enjoyed Yeti for Love!
Please consider leaving a review.

Sign up for my newsletter and get a free
ice cave sexy times bonus scene!www.nevapostau-
thor.com/yfl-bonus

Ready for some summer-time yeti? Check out Emma
and Yeshe's story in Rescued by Her Yeti.

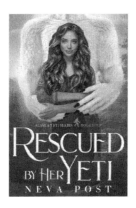

## A firefighting yeti who sets her heart aflame.

Despite dumping her boyfriend, Emma is still determined to go on her dream canoe trip in Alaska. The only problem? Everyone, including Yeshe—the hot wildland firefighting yeti she nearly flashes in a meet cute gone sideways—thinks she's on a couple's trip with her ex. But Emma is single, solo, and not going to let anything stop her. When she washes up alone on Yeshe's creek bank, she must come clean. Suddenly finding herself in strong, furry arms, she decides what happens on the creek, stays on the creek. But when their time is up, Emma craves more.

**A rebel in disguise who challenges his rule against love.**

Yeshe, has always avoided romantic relationships, never imagining his world would collide with a city girl like Emma. But from the moment their paths cross, he finds himself drawn to her independence, determination, and hidden tattoos—just how many does she have? When a twist of fate brings her to his remote cabin, Yeshe can't resist a short-term fling. However, when lust turns to love, Yeshe reminds her their time is up.

A short stint in Alaska and a rendezvous with a yeti is enough to convince Emma that North to the Future is a motto she can adopt, but can she convince Yeshe to let her in and take a chance on love?

"W hat did you call me?" Emma asked into
the awkward silence.

"Little bird." Sapphire eyes cut to her ink, now
covered by her tank top and hand. "You have a
sparrow tattoo on your side, under your arm."

Emma took a moment to calm her racing heart
and whirling mind. She'd been in Alaska less than a
day and might have flashed her boobs at a *yeti*, who
*immediately* noticed her body art. "It's small, hidden.
No one else knows. Please don't tell Gina. I'll never
hear the end of it."

Quirking his sky-blue lips, he made an X over his
chest. His *bare* chest. His shirt hung completely
open, exposing cut, furry pecs and abs that disappeared under the waistband of his work pants.

Emma did her best not to bite her lower lip. Yeti were her sister, Gina's thing, but... Wow.

"I won't tell," he said, then offered her his hand. "I'm Yeshe, by the way. Dorje's brother."

"Emma," she said, meeting his gaze in a serious, business-like manner—a mode she was most comfortable with—as if they were greeting each other over a boardroom table. At least until her palm slid into his, and her focus shifted to his huge blue hand gripping hers. His skin was equal parts rough, like a construction worker's might be, and smooth, like an old leather-bound book.

"I'm Gina's sister, but I think you know that." She quickly brought her gaze back to his face. Yeshe's white beard—or was that fur?—grew longer than Dorje's. Not unkempt, just a little...wild. Weathered blue cheeks spoke of time spent outdoors.

"Your eyes are a different color than your brother's," she mumbled as her gaze flit between each of those clear, deep, pools of blue. God, she'd never seen anything like Yeshe's eyes.

"Excuse me?" He slid his hand from hers.

Heat flushed her cheeks as embarrassment flooded through her. Why had she been studying his eyes so intently, and why had she commented on them? That wasn't a thing most people did during introductions. Could she be any more awkward? *Shake it off, Em.*

Emma backed up, crossing her arms over her chest again. But this time, she lifted her chin. If she didn't act like it was awkward, then it wouldn't be. "I was simply making an observation. I'd never seen a yeti before meeting Dorje—and now you. Your eyes are..." She swallowed down the embarrassment. "Striking." That was fine to say. It was true. Why deny it?

Yeshe grinned, making said eyes shine even brighter. "And I observe that your hair is darker than your sister's," he said.

Her hand glided up to the wavy strands, resembling a raven's nest at the moment. "It's brown."

Yeshe cocked his head and moved closer, ghosting his fingers over her unruly waves. "I'd call it mahogany."

Emma froze at his almost touch, holding her breath. She liked the intensity of his focus. She'd never been studied like this.

"You have beautiful streaks of red mixed with rich red-brown. Reminds me of a piece of wood I once worked."

She side-eyed Yeshe. Now that wasn't a comparison she'd ever received, but she oddly liked it coming from him. "Thank you, I think. My sister said you were in town to sell your wood carvings."

Yeshe buried his hands in his pants pockets. "I'm hoping to make a sales agreement."

"Good luck," Emma managed smothering a wide yawn. She pulled a towel from the rack. "Listen, I totally overslept. Gina might have mentioned to you that I'm in Alaska to go on a river trip? I'm surprised she didn't wake me up." She paused briefly and lowered her voice. "But it's really quiet upstairs. She and Dorje must still be asleep."

Yeshe's lips twitched, and it seemed like his eyes slid once more to her hair... No, to her eye mask. "Your sister and Dorje are still out. It's nearly ten o'clock—at night." He gestured toward the window. "Welcome to the Land of the Midnight Sun."

His words took a moment to sink in. Emma spun to look at the window, then snatched up her phone. Her gaze bounced from the timestamp on the phone's screen, to the light outside, then back to Yeshe, who appeared to be biting his lip so he wouldn't laugh. "Right. Well, I've never been this far north. This is new to me."

He offered a sympathetic smile. "I hear it happens to a lot of tourists."

Emma fought a swallow. "So I slept for an hour,

then barged in on you thinking it was morning and nearly took my shirt off."

Yeshe shrugged. "That sums it up. A memorable meeting."

Emma squeezed her eyes shut and grimaced. Memorable indeed.

———————

*Order your copy today!*

**Alaska Yeti Series:**

Ready for Her Yeti

Fake Dating Her Yeti

Yeti for Love

Catching Her Yeti

~ *Coming soon* ~

Rescued by Her Yeti

Married to Her Yeti

Loved by Her Yeti

## ACKNOWLEDGMENTS

As always, a huge thank you to my critique group. Heather, your extra read-throughs and advice are invaluable. Elizabeth, I don't know what I'd do without your input and editing expertise.

Scott, a million thank yous for your eagle eye and your never-ending patience when I need to finish just one more writerly task.

Kristin, thank you for your early read-through, feedback, and encouragement. Karen, I appreciate your early beta comments.

Lastly, thank you, reader, for your support and for loving yeti as much as I do.

# ABOUT THE AUTHOR

Neva Post grew up in a log house in Interior Alaska where she walked uphill both ways to school at temperatures of negative forty with only the aurora borealis to light her way. At least, that's how she remembers it.

She's equally happy on a snowy trail or coaxing vegetables to grow in her garden during the long Alaskan summer days. When she's not waxing skis or chasing voles out of her cabbage, she's at her computer. Neva's novels include paranormal elements—she can't help it—with smart and dependable characters who always get their HEA.

www.nevapostauthor.com

facebook.com/nevapostauthor

instagram.com/nevapostauthor

Made in the USA
Columbia, SC
16 September 2024

41476716R00138